# DISAR̲
# THE WILDEST
# WARRIOR

By Helen Louise Cox

Published in the United Kingdom by Helen Cox Books.

Copyright © 2020 by Helen Louise Cox.

Ebook ISBN: 978-1-8380221-7-4
Paperback ISBN: 978-1-8380221-8-1
Hardback ISBN: 978-1-8380801-0-5

Published in the United Kingdom by Helen Cox Books.

**Other Romance Titles by Helen Louise Cox**

Surrendering to the Gentleman Pirate
Once Upon a Rugged Knight

## *Historical Notes*

In 1725, when this story is set, the Shawnee nation are believed to have occupied West Virginia and Virginia, pushed east from the Ohio valley by the Iroquois nation. They would later be pushed west again by white settlers. I have depicted the Shawnee people as using the English language taught to them by English immigrants. At this point, indigenous people had more than a century of experience in translating between a wide range of Native and European languages.

The geography of Williamsburg is based on a map of the town as it stood in 1720. In the 18th Century, Europeans split their sleep into two segments. Thus, you will see references to 'second sleep' in this story.

# DISARMING THE WILDEST WARRIOR

BY HELEN LOUISE COX

# 1 7 2 5

## CHAPTER ONE

# Gilda

The heart-stopping howl of a man in torment was the first thing Gilda Griffiths heard when she stepped off the coach at Williamsburg. The next sound was pistol fire, loud enough and near enough to make the horses that had pulled them here from the James River whinny and rear. The coach driver steadied them, murmuring in hushed tones, while women, children and merchants selling their wares dashed for cover in nearby buildings. The few towns-men who had been milling around stopped whatever business they were conducting and set their sights on the corner of the market square nearest to where Gilda and her maid Arabella were standing.

The smoky scent of gunpowder drifted on the cool April breeze and Arabella nestled close to her mistress, crossing herself. Gilda, bracing for the worst, looked across to where all the men were staring. A bare-chested na-tive man, wearing nothing but buckskins, a leather belt and a breechcloth, stood just ten feet from them. Every muscle clenched in his firm body as he stared and puffed at a white man holding a large, bloodied knife. At first Gilda assumed the white man held the knife for protection but then got a hold on her faculties enough to notice an elderly native man lying on the dusty ground, still alive but bleeding badly. She studied the man wielding the knife. From here, it seemed he had scarce-ly a scratch on him. Had he stabbed the elderly native? If so, it had hardly been a fair fight. The man on the ground was so thin a strong wind might have knocked him down.

Another man dressed in a scarlet frock coat stood between the natives and their assailant. He held a pistol in each hand, one of them aloft his head.

'The next man to move gets the next bullet,' he spat, through his thick, auburn beard.

Gilda watched blood pool next to the elderly native. If sharp action wasn't taken he was going to die. In truth, even if he did receive medical attention his odds of survival didn't look good. But she had to try. Her father would want her to.

'Miss, where are you going?' Arabella said, with a note of alarm in her voice as she watched Gilda pick up her medicine bag in one hand and her dark green skirt in the other.

'To help. Come along now, don't dither.'

'You never said there'd be knives and pistols, Miss,' Arabella said following Gilda but at something of a distance. 'You didn't say there'd be sea-sickness neither.'

'You must think me in league with the devil to be able to predict such happenings, eh Bella?' Gilda said, slowing as she approached the men who were yet locked in their triangle of hostility.

'Ma'am,' the man with the gun addressed Gilda. 'I don't know if you have a death wish or somethin' but it's best you stay back lest you bloody your pretty little petticoats.'

The younger native turned to glare at her. By the ferocity flaring in his ocean blue eyes, it was clear he didn't welcome her presence any more than the man with the gun. Apparently a helping hand wasn't quite as welcome in the colony of Virginia as it had been back in Lincoln. As the native man turned to her head on, she realised the far side of his otherwise perfect face was pitted with scars along the cheekbone. From the look of them they were the lasting mark of smallpox. If Gilda's mother had lived through her afflictions she would no doubt have been left with the same reminder.

'I'm a physician,' Gilda said, tearing her eyes from the native's searing stare. She handed her bag to Arabella, pulled out a white apron that she carried rolled up in her pocket and began tying the cords around her waist.

'You, a doctor?' the white man with the knife slurred, before rocking his head back in laughter. 'A quack is more like it.'

Gilda raised an eyebrow at the square-faced hulk. She waited until he stopped snickering before speaking again. She wasn't going to be drowned out by some sweaty oaf who had probably never opened a book in his life, let alone read one.

'Easy there Lawson,' the man with the guns said to Williamsburg's resident cackling ape. 'I think you're offending Miss..?'

'Griffiths. Gilda Griffiths,' she said, while trying not to show surprise at how easily a name that didn't belong to her had rolled off her tongue. It seemed she had had enough practise at introducing herself as Gilda on the voyage here that the lie had stuck fast. 'And this is my maid, Arabella.'

'I'm the magistrate round here. Mr Charles Clarke.'

'How do you do Mr Clarke.' Gilda bobbed in a small curtsey and nudged Arabella to do the same. Privately, she admitted that a curtsey was a bit much. It's not as if Mr Clarke were royalty but Gilda needed to get by as best she could for the short time she was in Virginia and with that in mind it couldn't hurt to ingratiate herself with the local law enforcement. 'My father is a doctor back in England. He made me his apprentice. I'm more than qualified to treat this man and without my help, he will die.'

'So what?' said Lawson. The man looked as though he was having difficulty standing straight. He was bleeding here and there from small cuts he'd suffered in whatever struggle had taken place before the stabbing but, from the smell of him, his difficulty in sustaining proper balance had more to do with the whisky bottle than it did injury. 'He's a thieving old savage and he deserves to die.'

'That is not true. You've no proof,' the younger native growled before taking a single threatening step towards Lawson. Gilda noticed his triceps, emblazoned with a tribal tattoo, tighten as he did so. The obvious power in those muscles was… distracting.

'Hey, hey!' Mr Clarke warned, pointing his gun at the native. 'Keep your distance Blue Sky. I know your reputation.'

Gilda was left to wonder precisely what kind of reputation Mr Clarke was referring to as Blue Sky stood stock still and did not respond.

An agonizing groan came from the old man; his body writhing in the pain and dust.

Gilda looked down at him and then raised her eyebrows at Mr Clarke, making it clear, from her expression alone, that if this man died the loss was on him.

Pity flickered in Clarke's grey eyes as he glanced down at the wounded. 'Go on and help him, if you can.'

'What? That old thief stole three of my horses and you're just gonna –'

'If a village chief dies here today –'

'Village thief is more like it!'

'We're gonna invite trouble,' Mr Clarke cut back in, glancing towards the handful of townsmen still staring at the scene. 'And you know, Mr Lawson, how much I hate trouble. Besides, you got no proof so unless you want to see me in court about that man's wound I suggest you come along and let the lady work.'

Lawson eyed Mr Clarke, Blue Sky, Arabella and Gilda in turn before sneering: 'Since you're going to help the half-breed's father, you may as well help your fellow white man too.' Before Mr Clarke could stop him, Lawson grabbed a handful of Gilda's apron and used it to clean his bloody knife.

Arabella let out an outraged gasp but Gilda didn't flinch.

Granted, Lawson was doing all he could to humiliate her. But if he thought that was the worst she'd ever suffered at the hands of a man, he was gravely mistaken. She already knew his type. The last thing she was going to do was give him the satisfaction of believing he was in any way intimidating.

'That's it, you're stinkin' drunk. You're going to sit in the gaolhouse 'till you've shaken it off.' Mr Clarke said, grabbing Lawson by the scruff of his neck. 'Apologies Ma'am,' he added, touching the brim of his hat before shoving a muttering Lawson off to pay his penance. As they stumbled away the other men who had been watching the show from a safe distance also slowly dispersed.

The moment Gilda was sure Lawson would be no more hindrance, she turned back to the elderly man. He was twisting in agony and in the time it had taken to argue his right to care he had lost a lot more blood. It seemed there wasn't going to be any official justice for what Lawson had done so the least Gilda could do was try to minimise the old man's suffering. She struggled to keep her expression neutral as she knelt beside him for fear that he would use some ancient shaman's trick to see the truth in her eyes: that it was probably already too late to save his life.

## CHAPTER TWO

# Blue Sky

'We cannot pay you,' Blue Sky snapped as the woman who called herself Gilda started to unpack items strange and unfamiliar from the big black bag her maid held open.

'Just as well I did not ask for payment then.'

'We don't need your help,' Blue Sky tried again.

At his remark, Gilda sighed in such a way that her full bosom heaved against the laced garments the women of the town always wore. To Blue Sky's eyes these clothes usually looked like just another cage the white people had built for themselves but the way the material clasped Gilda's curves made it difficult to concentrate on making his usual distaste for her kind clear. She brushed away a blonde curl that had escaped her white cap and stared up at him. Her eyes were blue like his. In truth, not exactly like his. His were named after the summer sky whereas hers were better named after the Turquoise stone in a bracelet his mother had made for him when he was young.

'Blue Sky…' she breathed out his name in a soft, husky tone that squeezed at something inside. 'Do you love your father?'

He frowned down at her for a long moment before answering. 'Of course.'

'Then let me try to save him.'

'Blue Sky, let her please,' his father groaned.

Gilda turned back to the old man, put a hand on his cheek and smiled.

'Good, you're still with me.'

His father made an expression that if he hadn't been in so much pain would have been a smile.

Blue Sky silenced at his father's request. But he had seen too much treachery from her kind to be so easily fooled. What trick was this woman playing in offering to heal his father? White people didn't heal his kind, they exploited them, attacked them and slaughtered them. Or, at least, they had before he had become his people's fiercest brave. From the moment he had been old enough to hold a bow, he had begun teaching white people it was best to leave his village alone. As such, save the likes of Lawson, most local settlers had learned to treat the Shawnee with cold disinterest.

Even now the good people of the town had gone back to their business, uncaring that his father lay bleeding, likely dying, at the edge of the market square. Blue Sky wasn't surprised by their indifference. White people even slaughtered their own kind if they could find a reason to.

When Gilda nursed his father however, her manner was gentle; full of tenderness. Why? She did not know them. What did she gain from administering aid?

'Bella, alcohol,' Gilda instructed, before inspecting the wound.

Blue Sky, trying not to breathe in the intoxicating scent of freshly cut roses that seemed to emanate from her every pore, leaned over her so he could see how badly his father was hurt.

'The wound is wide, but it's not too deep,' Gilda said. 'I've seen men come back from worse.'

Blue Sky didn't speak but his frown deepened. He should have killed Lawson on the spot for this. He should have killed him for his ill-treatment of women alone. When he had grabbed at Gilda's skirt, Blue Sky had almost grabbed Lawson's throat. That man was an animal and Blue Sky intended to kill him like one. But he couldn't have his revenge now. Not when he and his injured father were outnumbered by their enemy, most of whom owned pistols. He would have to wait but in good time he would spill Lawson's blood, the same way Lawson had spilled his father's.

Arabella's green eyes were hard with concentration as she rooted through the bag and produced a bottle and a piece of material. Pouring some liquid onto the rag, Gilda said: 'What is your name, sir?'

'You would call me Great Hawk,' Blue Sky's father replied.

'Great Hawk,' Gilda repeated, keeping her voice soft and holding up the now soaked rag. 'This might hurt. But it's good. You understand?'

'He understands,' snapped Blue Sky. 'He's been speaking English longer than you.'

Ignoring Blue Sky's comment, Gilda pressed the rag against the wound. Great Hawk winced and cried out in pain. Gilda took hold of his hand and squeezed it, giving the liquid a moment to work its magic before removing it.

'Will you be wanting the needle, Miss?' said Arabella.

'I'm afraid so,' Gilda said, accepting a needle and thread from her maid.

'What are you going to do with that?' asked Blue Sky.

'Help me move him onto his side, will you?' Gilda responded with a tender smile that Blue Sky did not want to trust. After a few moments of hesitation he decided he had little other choice and obliged.

Great Hawk cried out again as Gilda started the first stitch. 'I'm sorry,' she said.

On the seventh stitch Great Hawk's body fell limp and his breath became shallow.

'What have you done?'

'He's fainted that's all,' said Arabella, placing both hands on her slender hips in what Blue Sky deemed a rather over-confident manner given his father's lifeless form. ''Appens to the best of us,' she added, her voice a little quieter in response to his hardened stare.

'It's probably better this way, he won't feel anything,' Gilda assured him.

Once she had finished the stitches, Gilda cut a long piece of linen from a roll she pulled out of her bag and with Blue Sky's help she wrapped the fabric tight around Great Hawk's stomach, securing it with a pin. By the time they had finished a diverting blush glowed in Gilda's cheeks from the effort it had taken. It was a dangerous detail Blue Sky was keen to disregard. Her face had turned the deep pink he imagined her whole body would be after he'd laid her down in the grassy plains: her laces undone and her petticoats hitched high above her thighs.

'How far is your home from here?' Gilda asked, mercifully interrupting his unwanted thoughts.

'Why?'

'Because he should not travel any further than necessary in his condition.'

'Our village is not far north from here.'

Gilda nodded. 'I will need to visit him to check on and remove the stitches. I am only in Virginia for two weeks but that should be long enough to make sure he's healed.'

Blue Sky remained silent. A strange ache surfaced in his chest at the mention of her leaving so soon. He did not understand the white-hot pulse carving through him. He only knew he didn't want to experience it any more than he wanted her visiting the village.

The Shawnee had learned to be careful about who they invited into their homes. In order to avoid giving her any sign that she would be welcomed by his people, he focused on lifting his father in his arms. He was about to walk away when some unidentifiable urge forced him to speak.

'I suppose I owe you thanks,' he ground out as Arabella started packing away Gilda's supplies.

Gilda stood, dusted off her apron and shook her head. 'You owe me no thanks.'

'Why not?'

'My reasons are my own,' Gilda replied. 'But in the short time I'm here, whatever aid I offer to you or your people, you will owe me no thank you.'

Blue Sky looked at Gilda side-long, sensing some kind of trap. Had she done something to Great Hawk? Something that would only speed his death? If not, why did she shun his gratitude?

Great Hawk's eyes fluttered open as Blue Sky prepared to carry him away.

'Wait,' he said.

Against his better judgment, Blue Sky obeyed and watched his father reach out a shaky hand and cup Gilda's face.

'I will call you Little Sun,' he said to her. 'Because like the sun you give life.'

Blue Sky could see tears in Gilda's eyes as she pressed her own hand against his father's, his sun-weathered skin so dark next to hers whiter than the moon. 'That's the first time in my life anyone has called me little,' Gilda said.

Arabella, who had finished tidying up, snickered. 'I'd put ten shillings on that, Miss.'

Great Hawk again tried to smile.

'Little Sun... It has more poetry than my given name, thank you,' she added.

Great Hawk fought for a moment to keep his eyes open but again drifted into a blank sleep.

'Blue Sky,' Gilda whispered, keeping one eye on Great Hawk to be sure he couldn't hear her. 'I've done all I know to do for your father but he may not yet live. Keep him warm. If he even looks as though he might be starting a fever, call for me at once. I'm to reside on Queen Street. I have yet to see the property for myself but it's owned by the Widow Westerby and I believe the house is yellow. Understood?'

Blue Sky didn't respond. The son of a village chief didn't take orders from a white woman, or any of their kind.

'Understood?' she repeated, this time more sharply. Her manner had been so gentle up until this point that Blue Sky blinked in surprise. How could blue eyes have fire in them? It seemed impossible. Yet when he looked into hers that was what he saw. He scowled as he caught himself wondering what could fuel such a fire in her.

Blue Sky offered a stiff nod to acknowledge what she had said. He had no further time for quarrel. His father needed rest and the healing of his people.

Turning his back on her, he stalked his way out of the market square, carrying his father towards their horse and willing himself not to look back in Gilda's direction no matter how inviting a sight she may be.

While checking his father was secure in the travois, Blue Sky tried to decide what kind of swindle Gilda had just played. Healing his father without payment or thanks must be part of some bigger plan. But what kind? Mounting his black horse, and setting off back to the village Blue Sky made a solemn promise that no matter what the obstacles he would find out.

# CHAPTER THREE

usk was casting its velvet spell by the time Gilda and Arabella turned the corner of Queen Street. They had arrived late in the day and most vendors who frequented the market square had already gone home. They did, however, purchase goods from the few merchants left standing.

After seventy-five days of nothing but fish, salted beef and sea biscuits it had proven impossible to resist buying a handful of fresh strawberries which were, to Gilda's recollection, the best thing she had ever tasted. Arabella made short work of hers too. Gilda had been doubly pleased to purchase some flour, eggs, butter and a few other items. The modest selection of goods would save her from arriving empty-handed to Widow Westerby – an old patient of her father's who had agreed to provide shelter, and a welcome re-spite, between an almost-three month voyage and their thousand mile expedition to New Orleans. Another thousand miles on top of the four thousand they had already travelled would surely be sufficient distance to keep Gilda safe from *him*.

The merchants in the square had been pos-itively fervent to swap their goods for Gilda's British pounds. Unfortunately, for change they had bestowed an assortment of poor quality coinage she hadn't even recognised. She was taking it on trust they hadn't relieved her of more money than they should. She would show the coins to Widow Westerby. Hopefully she would be able to shed light on this unexpected aspect of life in the colony.

'Thought it must be you when I saw you turn the corner,' the woman she presumed to be Widow Westerby said as Gilda approached the threshold of the only yellow house on Queen Street. The white-haired lady sat on an upturned metal canister knitting a pair of stockings.

Gilda smiled. 'Is it so very obvious that we're new here?'

'No, but you've got your father's nose,' Widow Westerby said, setting her knitting aside.

'Why Goodie Westerby, are you implying my nose is so big it's visible from the end of the street?'

'No, child, no,' the old woman said before letting out a breathy cackle that took such hold of her she almost fell off her make-shift seat. After a moment she righted herself and stood to greet her guests.

'How do you do, Ma'am,' said Arabella, bowing her head of loose chestnut curls while holding up a basket of goods. 'Mistress bought you some food on the way here. It's just as well, she likes her food, she does.' Widow Westerby cleared her throat, clearly unsure about how to respond to Arabella's somewhat insolent comment. For the first seven days of their Atlantic voyage Gilda had reproached Arabella for such remarks. After that however she realised Arabella wasn't in-solent at all. She just hadn't been in line when tact was portioned out. Consequently, she had taken to ignoring her maid's occasional boldness and focussed instead on her good qualities.

'This is Bella,' said Gilda. 'Give her half a chance and I promise she'll be more help than hindrance to you while we're here.'

'I thank you for the food,' Widow Westerby said at last. 'From what I hear you've picked up a reputation as well as some eggs on your short walk from town. Made quite the impression on Mr Clarke, I believe.'

Gilda's mouth dropped open. 'How did news of that reach you before we did?'

Widow Westerby put her hands on Gilda's shoulders and then cupped her cheeks in her hands. 'You'll find there're no secrets here, child. Everybody knows everybody, and everybody's business.'

Gilda was pretty sure from the tone that Widow Westerby meant to frame this as a comforting fact of life in Williamsburg. Instead, Gilda's shoulders clenched. How long would it be, she wondered, before the good folk of Virginia started to ask questions about why she left England? Why, at the ripe age of twenty-seven, she was without husband or family? Her father had told Widow Westerby enough for her to understand Gilda's need to leave England urgently and adopt a new name. The old lady had been sworn to secrecy about the little he had told her but there was still so much she didn't know, and Gilda would prefer it to stay that way.

She had a story prepared before she even bought her ticket to America and tried it out when she had hired Arabella. Her maid had seemed satisfied enough with what Gilda had told her: that she did not wish to stay in England and marry an old man who smelled of brandy and snuff. Instead, she explained, she intended to cross the Atlantic in search of some greater fortune in the New World. But Arabella, orphaned and working for some powdered old woman on the outskirts of London, was more interested in asking about what life would be like in America than interrogating Gilda's reasons for leaving merry old England. From what Widow Westerby said, the locals here would be much more probing.

Still, she only had to hold off their curiosity for a fortnight. If the questions became too personal, they could simply leave sooner.

'I had hoped to see you a little more than a week ago,' Widow Westerby said, breaking into Gilda's thoughts.

'Our ship was thrown off course by an unexpected current,' Gilda explained. 'We were aboard the Royal Charles a good ten days longer than expected.'

'Thought it must've been something like that,' Widow Westerby said with a nod. 'I remember from my crossing some fifteen years ago now that seafaring is an uncertain business. But I must admit when this letter arrived before you turned up, I couldn't help but worry some.'

Widow Westerby reached into her skirt pocket and pulled out a letter. It was addressed to Gilda and she at once recognised the handwriting as that belonging to her brother, Andrew.

'He must have sent it on a faster ship than the one I boarded,' Gilda said, a pang of home-sickness pulsing through her at the sight of his familiar hand. She raised her eyebrow at the envelope, which had the word SHIP marked across the back in large letters, before pocketing it.

'Aren't you going to read it, Mistress?' said Arabella, the note of curiosity in her voice utterly giving her away.

'Later,' Gilda replied. 'Today has been the longest day of my life so far, I think, and I am in need of rest.'

'Come on inside,' said Widow Westerby turning to pick up her knitting. 'The beds I've made up for you are comfortable enough. We've a healthy larder and if you need transport to anyplace local, Mr Brownlow, who has the good fortune of being my neighbour, has a stable out back with a couple of horses. He'll be able to arrange a carriage for you with a day's notice. Luckily for us, he's happy to be paid in cider and cornbread.'

Gilda was doing her utmost to listen to what Widow Westerby was saying but an uneasy feeling came over her. A sense of being watched. Was that whisky she could smell?

'Evenin' ladies,' said a slimy but familiar voice.

'Mr Lawson,' Widow Westerby said, turning to greet him.

Gilda's stomach tightened. Wasn't he supposed to be in gaol sobering up? Perhaps Mr Clarke had had enough of the ape and turned him out.

'Are you well? I hear you had an awful skirmish with the natives,' said Widow Westerby.

That's one way of describing what happened, Gilda thought. And then, not for the first time that afternoon, she found herself again remembering the depths of Blue Sky's ocean eyes. She'd had such an odd feeling when he stared at her, as though he'd known how she looked with neither petticoat nor shift. It wasn't just his eyes that stuck in her memory though. She remembered again the dark silk of his hair, so much more appealing than the powdered wigs favoured by most of the men back in England. The soft bronze of his chest hadn't escaped her notice either. Nor the way his muscles formed in chevrons that pointed down to all that lay hidden behind his breechcloth.

How old must he be? Twenty-four, perhaps twenty-five? Was that old enough to develop the kind of stamina she imagined him capable of?

'I have a few complaints,' Lawson said, cutting through a fancy Gilda would rather have held onto. Instead it seemed she had no choice but to converse with a man whose behaviour had been nothing short of vile since the moment they met. 'Those savages sure know how to fight, I'll give them that. Truth of the matter is, I came to apologise to Miss Griffiths. I don't recall the details, but Mr Clarke said I was unseemly to the lady and I've come to ask your forgiveness on the matter. I've been told I can get pretty mean when I've had too much whisky.'

Gilda nodded but did not offer Lawson a smile. She didn't believe for a second he'd forgotten what he'd done just a few hours prior, no matter how much whisky he'd had. After that trick with the knife and her apron, Mr Clarke had probably threatened him with some kind of penalty if he didn't settle the matter. She wouldn't so easily forgive what he had done to Great Hawk, who seemed such a gentle man, but she wasn't going to make an outright enemy of a violent drunk either. It wasn't worth it when she and Arabella would be gone in two weeks.

'I thank you for taking the time to apologise for your actions,' Gilda said. 'It takes a courageous man to admit when his behaviour has been out of line. We all make mistakes Mr Lawson.'

Lawson removed his hat and held it humbly in his hands revealing a head of greasy blonde hair that Gilda was pretty sure hadn't been washed since the turn of the century. 'I was wonderin' if you'd be so kind as to tend my wounds Miss Griffiths. I'm sure with you fine-lookin' ladies to nurse me I'll heal all the quicker after what that dirty savage did to me.'

Gilda found herself wishing Blue Sky and Great Hawk had done a little more damage to Lawson before he pulled a knife on them. It was a thought that startled her. As a doctor's daughter she had always been taught it was not her place to decide who deserved to be healed; who lived or died. Only God could decide that.

'Won't you sit down Mr Lawson?' Gilda said, deciding the least she could do to make up for the sheer number of wayward thoughts she had indulged in that day was to treat someone she would rather not.

'I'll go and fix you all some cider while you tend Mr Lawson,' said Widow Westerby, before disappearing inside.

Lawson sat on the upturned canister and Arabella opened Gilda's medical bag.

Without any of the tenderness or warning she'd offered Great Hawk, Gilda soaked a fresh rag and pressed alcohol into Lawson's wounds.

'Yow!' Lawson said, jumping a few inches out of his seat.

'Why Mr Lawson,' said Gilda, pressing a hand against her chest in feigned dismay. 'Forgive me. I've never had a patient who found the alcohol so painful.'

'No, I-I-I was just kiddin', I was just kiddin' now,' Lawson said. 'It was a surprise is all.'

Arabella covered her mouth in an attempt not to laugh. When Lawson wasn't looking, Gilda shot her a wicked smile as she continued to dab various cuts while Lawson sucked through his teeth.

She knew these weren't the actions of a righteous woman but perhaps after all she had suffered back in England, God would be gracious enough to permit her a little fun out here in America. She had, after all, vowed to make the most of every day here. Contemplating that thought further she couldn't help but wonder if her blue-eyed native might play some part in those hedonistic adventures, even if only for a little while.

# CHAPTER FOUR

The red cardinals had long-ceased their almost sorrowful chirping and the full pink moon was high amongst the stars when Blue Sky saw Gilda steal out of the yellow house on Queen Street. Her movements seemed strange, agitated almost. She was a different creature to the collected medicine woman who had treated his father earlier that day. He watched as she sneaked around the row of houses before reappearing a short while later on a tawny horse, her legs astride the beast in a manner he would never have expected from the other townswomen. She tapped the beast lightly with her foot and rode off into the darkness, her long, blonde mane, with no cap to conceal it, flying free behind her.

Slinking from the foliage he had used as camouflage to the area near The Capitol, Blue

Sky hastily untethered his horse from a tree and mounted to give chase. After a long evening of patient scouting, this was his chance to find out the truth about Gilda Griffiths.

When delivering Great Hawk back to his village, he had waited just long enough to see his father open his eyes. The moment he was assured he would stay awake sooner than die, Blue Sky instructed his most trusted ally: Fast River, to watch over Great Hawk while he rode straight back to town. There he hid, out of sight, watching and waiting. Gilda had said herself that she did not know if Great Hawk would live and if he died it would be left to Blue Sky to protect the lives of his Shawnee brethren from the whites. With that in mind, it was vital he learned as much as he could about this new potential menace.

Gilda had spent most of her time on the porch that afternoon caught in some dreamy gaze and he had wondered more than once what or who she was thinking of. The highlight of his vigil however had been her taunting of Lawson about his reaction to her physician's tricks. She was wily. Lawson did not even realise she was mocking him. But experience told Blue Sky that Gilda's sharp edge was cause for caution, even in spite of her seeming mildness. Perhaps she was a spy for the settlers, and planned to infiltrate his village through pretended kindness only to report back on his people's weapons and their weaknesses.

He had been sure that if he kept watch long enough she would do something to give herself away, and now here she was in the dead of night riding unchaperoned in the direction of what had, under white rule, come to be known as the James River. No virtuous lady of the town would be out alone at this time of night. He didn't know her darker purpose but if he remained far enough behind, and undetected, he was certain it would reveal itself soon.

At the pace she was riding, it didn't take her long to reach the river. Blue Sky surveyed Gilda as she tethered her horse then secured his own steed out of sight. She was not dressed for sleep. She wore the same green dress as earlier but she was without a shawl, as though she had left in a hurry and forgotten it. She shivered in the coolness of the night and for a moment all he could think of was cocooning her creamy body in his to warm her through. Cursing, he shook himself out of the day-dream at once and crept closer to the edge of the riverbank where she now stood. He took every precaution not to rustle even a single leaf so as not to alert her to his presence.

What happened next, he was not prepared for.

As he neared, he realised the woman was sobbing. Not gentle, silent tears but deep gut-wrenching wails that shook a person's shoulders with thundering might. She fell to her knees as if kneeling before the Great Spirit himself, and beat her fists against the ground.

'Dad!' she screamed to the unhearing night stars. She screamed this word over and over again. Each time the word sounded more desperate and her breath more ragged. Blue Sky knew this word. It was how white people referred to their fathers.

Had something happened to Little Sun's father? There had been no man with her when she treated Great Hawk. Lawson was the only man to be seen at the yellow house and he had begrudgingly left before sunset. The only other notion Blue Sky had was that Little Sun's father was far away and she had heard bad news about him. The mere sight of her tortured anguish was enough to rouse the protector in him and he stood, poised to go to her, hold her and shield her.

But then, almost as quick, Blue Sky halted and scowled as he realised he had thought about this woman as Little Sun. That he had almost given his position away and gone to comfort his conniving enemy at the first test of his resolve. He must not let whatever grief she suffered fool him into seeing her as anything other than what she was: one of them. They took his mother away. Killed her for nothing more than sport and cruelty. He was glad if Gilda's father had been taken away. Why shouldn't she know his pain?

'Forgive me father,' Gilda whispered to the river, slowly rocking her body from side to side as a mother might rock a baby in her arms. 'I love you. Please forgive me.'

She wept this way for a little while longer. Almost long enough for Blue Sky to feel shameful about wishing her father away.

Almost, but not quite.

Once she had finished weeping she dusted off her skirt and turned back to the horse who was huffing his cloudy breath into the night air. Gilda stroked the horse's nose.

'I'm glad you're here, girl,' she said to the horse. 'I couldn't let Bella or Goodie Westerby hear me cry like that but I'd rather I weren't alone right now.'

Spurred by an unexpected sense of compassion that had not surfaced in as long as he could remember, not even when his white captives had begged him for release after a battle, Blue Sky stepped from the shadows. And before he could stop his lips he heard himself say, in a soothing voice that did not in the least resemble his own: 'You are not alone.'

# CHAPTER FIVE

ilda spun around at the unexpected deep voice. When she saw who it belonged to, her breath hitched. There he stood: man who, before she had read Andrew's letter, had occupied her thoughts for most of the evening. Looking at him, it wasn't difficult to understand why he had so instantly and completely captured her imagination. His bared muscles granted him a striking silhouette in the near darkness. His long, inky hair was tied in a knot atop his head. His eyes shimmered in the moonlight. There was an untold story in those eyes. She had known that even on their first meeting, earlier that day, in the market place. His eyes had flickered with tacit suffering then just as they did now. Perhaps it was her doctor's instincts, but she wished, not for the first time, that she could find a way to ease that unspoken agony.

'Blue Sky,' she gasped. Drying her eyes, she took several steps towards him. 'What brings you here? Is it your father? Does he have a fever?'

Blue Sky studied her a long moment and took a step closer. 'He is healing,' he said at last. 'I was out riding when I heard you.'

Gilda looked briefly at the ground before raising her chin once more. 'I am sorry. I believed I would be out of earshot here. I didn't mean to startle you.'

'It takes more than that to startle a Shawnee warrior,' he said. 'We are trained to be fearless.'

'Is that so?'

'Yes. I only came to see for myself you were not in any physical peril.'

Gilda shook her head. 'As you can see, I am not.'

'But you are… hurting,' Blue Sky said inching close enough for Gilda to breathe in the stirring scent of wood smoke and cedar drifting from him.

Gilda frowned, wondering whether to confide. Up until now Blue Sky had made it clear he had no time or fondness for her, even while she healed his ailing father. And why should he? She was a stranger and life out here was hard, even more so for his kind. Perhaps it was her obvious distress that had brought out his gentle side. But if he was merely conversing with her out of a sense of duty or pity she didn't wish to burden him.

'I am in some distress, but I shall live through it,' she said at last, managing a small smile.

'Is your father in some kind of trouble?'

Gilda's smile dwindled. So he had not only heard her crying, he had witnessed her most desperate pleas. Those that she had hoped would carry down the James River, out across to the Atlantic and all the way back to the cemetery at St Mary Magdalene's Church in Lincoln, where her father now surely lay. 'My brother Andrew sent a letter from England informing me that my father… that he passed on, the day after I set sail for America.'

'I am sorry,' said Blue Sky, his voice level but not completely unfeeling.

Gilda nodded her acknowledgment. 'I knew there was a chance I may not see him again when I left but it was enough to know he was out there in the world somewhere. Looking up at the same moon I was. But now he's… he's gone, and I was not there for him in his final hours.'

Gilda thought she had got all the weeping out of her system, at least for now, but without warning her whole body shook as she gave into her grief once more. Blue Sky reached out a tentative hand and squeezed Gilda's shoulder but she was so much in distress that this level of contact simply wasn't enough. Without a second thought she wrapped her arms around Blue Sky's torso and rested her head against his firm chest. Gilda knew it was a liberty but she couldn't help herself. Being so far away from anyone she might ordinarily turn to at a time like this was unbearable.

Several moments passed before she felt Blue Sky's muscles relax. Slowly, his arms encircled her and in the space of a few more heartbeats his roughened hands were stroking her hair. The motion was pacifying, as was the strength of Blue Sky's arms. When he locked them about her she felt a wave of unexpected relief. She knew she could not stay like this for any length of time. That if anyone from the town happened to be riding by her reputation would be in ruins. And who knows what the men of the town would do to Blue Sky for touching a white woman? But while he embraced her it seemed no harm could reach her. Not the bitter truth of her father's passing nor the haunting misdeeds of the dark, violent figure she had escaped when she left for the New World.

Once her sobs had subsided, she slowly raised her head. Her face was just inches from Blue Sky's. So near, she could feel the warmth of his breath against her cheeks. The traces of cedar she had caught earlier were more potent from this proximity. He was all she was breathing in.

She stared up at him with wide eyes. For the first time since they had met, she was close enough to study his face in detail. She noticed a heavy line in the middle of his forehead that betrayed the fact he frowned too much and his firm lips, which she began to imagine covering with her own, were framed by dark stubble. He stared at her in return, unflinching; unmoving.

Slowly, she felt her mouth moving towards his. Blue Sky didn't pull away. Nor did he lean towards her. He remained still except for his breathing which was tremulous and deep. As if he, like her, was at once unsettled and exhilarated by the prospect of their inevitable collision. The moment their lips met, Gilda was overwhelmed by the most unusual sensation. The rest of the world seemed to drop away into some dark abyss, leaving only the two of them. Only softness. Only warmth.

Surprised by the tender intensity of his kiss, Gilda opened her lips wider to receive his tongue and as she did so Blue Sky tightened his grip on her. Gilda felt her whole body weaken at being held so fiercely. He held her as though she were the only other being in existence.

In response, she crushed her mouth harder against his until their tongues touched, and tangled. He leaned his body against hers and she pushed back against him just as hard, certain, in that moment, that no matter how much they pressed themselves to one another, it would never quite feel close enough. His hands slid slowly down her back, squeezing when they reached her bottom. Moaning into his mouth at the boldness of this gesture, she arched her body further into his to make sure there was no mistaking her attraction to him. Her eyes widened as she realised his want for her was just as ardent; proven by an unmissable stiffness straining behind his breechcloth.

Aroused by the thought that this striking man craved her in all the most primal ways, Gilda began to drive her hips against his coupling this action with what could only be described as a desperate whimper. At this, he clasped her bottom harder and lifted her an inch or two from the ground, just enough to better align the parts of them that most betrayed their craving for each other. She grazed his bared back with her fingernails and her legs threatened to rise and wrap themselves around his waist. It was only then that Gilda was struck by how far and how quickly the situation had developed.

What was she doing?

Forcing herself on a man who had made his contempt for her more than clear, that's what.

Much against her will, she abruptly broke the kiss and pulled away.

'Oh, Blue Sky, I'm so very sorry,' Gilda said, trying to catch her breath. She didn't dare look into his eyes in case she forgot herself again. 'You must think me such a manipulative wretch,' she said, not pausing for an answer but in her embarrassment talking twenty words to the second. 'You have made it clear that you have no fondness for me. Despite that, you tried to comfort me when you found out I was in pain and I – I – I am not myself.' She steeled herself to look at him then. His expression was unreadable in the near-darkness. 'I hope you can find it in your heart to forgive me. It will not happen again, I assure you.'

Was that disappointment flickering in his eyes? Or was that simply what she wanted to see?

'It's forgotten,' he said at last.

'Thank you,' she said, trying not to let the discontent sound out in her tone. The idea that she would never again taste the pleasure she had just sampled was not an agreeable one. But he was acting under duress, out of pity. And that was not fitting. 'As a physician who is, at present, caring for your father I want you to feel safe around me.'

Blue Sky laughed in a manner that almost sounded almost sardonic to Gilda's ears. 'Most of the townsfolk would say it is your safety that is at risk right now, not mine.'

'Yes, well. That's because the townsfolk of Williamsburg don't know how good I am in a fight. You think you're fearless? Try being a little sister to a man with fists the size of small boulders. You soon learn to defend yourself under those circumstances.'

'The victory would still be mine,' Blue sky said, smirking.

'I would not count on that if I were you,' Gilda said, making her way back to the horse. 'My instincts are just as sharp as – as, Blue Sky?' Gilda looked all about her but the native had vanished in an instant. Guessing his game, she smiled to herself and continued the walk back to her ride. 'Oh, dear me, Blue Sky must have gone back to his village,' she said, expecting to hear a rustle in the grasses somewhere nearby, giving away his hiding place. When nothing stirred after a minute, Gilda frowned. Maybe Blue Sky really had just disappeared? If so, how foolish of her to think he was being playful. After his attitude towards her in the market square that afternoon why should she assume he would suddenly want to lark around with her? Even after that kiss. One she would never forget.

Shrugging, she took a few more steps towards the horse only to be knocked sideways with incredible might. The blow was enough to take her clean off her feet and yet she felt no pain at all as she rolled into the grass, cradled in Blue Sky's arms. Gilda exploded with laughter at the surprise, something that just a short while ago she had been sure she would never do again.

When they finally came to a stop, Blue Sky lay on top of her, panting and staring down into her face, his eyes dropped and fixed on her mouth. There was no argument about it: he was beautiful. Even the scar on his cheek somehow made him more appealing. If she had not promised never to kiss him again but three minutes ago she would have leaned into him and forgot the world again.

But then, she remembered that she had been deceived by a beautiful face before. By a gruff, strong jawline and eyes darker than the depths of the ocean she had crossed to elude him. Recalling how much that man had cost her, Gilda indicated that she wanted to sit up.

Blue Sky obliged at once.

'I think the safest thing for both of us just now is to go home,' she said, ensuring her voice was as warm and gentle as she could make it. The last thing she wanted was for Blue Sky to feel rejected, especially as she had been the one to kiss him.

Blue Sky nodded and offered her his hand. She took it and pulled herself up.

'I will ride to the edge of the town with you. A lady like yourself cannot be careful enough.

There are plenty of undesirables out here. I should know, I am one of them.'

Gilda chuckled and shook her head at him as she went to untether her horse. After feeling his heat and intensity first-hand, undesirable is the last word she would ever use to describe Blue Sky.

# CHAPTER SIX

Four days passed before Blue Sky had any business visiting Gilda Griffiths. Four endless days of busying himself with hunting, fishing and shooting arrows into practice marks so he might forget the fire that had at once ignited within when she threw her arms around him and nestled her precious little head into his chest. Five near-torturous nights of lying awake, thinking about how close he had been to tearing at her laces and freeing those plentiful breasts which he imagined to be fuller than the moon. How many times he had wished he had taken his chance while she lay beneath him in the long Virginian grass and made her shapely form writhe until his name was the only word she could remember. Though he had filled his time with every imaginable distraction, nothing cooled his want for her. Not even stroking the length of himself, while imagining his hands were hers.

Despite his undeniable urge to know just how loudly she screamed when she climaxed, it would not have been right to seduce her that night. Not when she was grieving for her father. He knew the pain of losing a parent better than anyone and there was no honour in exploiting a woman that way.

Before she left Virginia however, he would, he had decided, make her want him and not because she was grieving or afraid or lonely. By the time he was through with his seduction, she would beg to feel him deep inside her. He had never looked the way of a white woman before and he didn't plan to make it a habit. A night of wanton pleasure with her would cure him of these impulses and then she would be gone. After that, so long as she agreed to take the right medicine to prevent a baby, he would not have to think on her, or any other white woman, again.

Five nights ago he had bid her goodbye at the edge of town and promised to return this morning to report on his father's health.

She believed he had left her to find her own way home then. In truth, he followed her at a distance back to the yellow house. That way, he could be certain she was safe without any of the toothless town gossips seeing him standing on her porch just before sunrise and drawing their own spiteful conclusions. Regardless of the way his body throbbed for hers, he knew better than to ruin her reputation. The Shawnee understood the need for young men and women to experiment with each other's bodies. This was not a sentiment the white man shared.

From his hiding place that night he had watched her hips sway back towards the yellow house, back towards the world he could never be a part of. In that moment Blue Sky had at last admitted to himself that he wanted to lie with Little Sun. If she was half as passionate in her carnal duties as she was in her kiss then it would be worth his time to entice her. She had paused at the door and he could tell, even with the distance between them, that she was again weeping for her lost father. It took every ounce of will not to go to her then. To sweep her up in his arms and use every trick he could think of to make her forget her pain. Mercifully, she went inside before his resolve crumbled.

Now, having dismounted and tethered his horse at the end of Queen Street, he walked towards the yellow house and noticed Arabella sitting on the porch with a book.

'Mistress says she'll be down shortly,' Arabella said, when she noticed him approach. 'Suppose I'd best keep you company 'till then.'

Arabella wore a strange, over-familiar smile that brought Blue Sky deep discomfort. Had Gilda told her about what they had shared? Gossiping about her brush with the Indian? Had they laughed about him? Though his muscles tensed at the thought he reminded himself he would laugh longest when she begged him to take her.

'I'd rather look at you than the pages of that book I borrowed from Mistress,' Arabella added.

Though Great Hawk had taught him to speak English well, Blue Sky could only read a small amount and the words on the book cover were beyond him.

'What is the book?' he asked, doing his best to sound as though it was of no consequence to him whether Arabella told him what it pleased Little Sun to read.

'*A Journal of the Plague Year*,' said Arabella. 'It's about disease. You would think Mistress would want to ponder something else from time to time, but all the volumes she brought are boring medical books. Hence why I'm so glad you're 'ere.'

Arabella stood from her seat on an upturned canister and took a few steps towards Blue Sky, not stopping until she was much closer than he would like.

'You've got an 'andsome face, 'aven't you?'

'I had not noticed,' Blue Sky lied. He knew his face was no hardship to the women who crossed his path. He didn't lie down with just any woman but none that he had wanted had denied him. Little Sun wouldn't deny him either, he would make sure of it.

''Cept for those scars, eh?' Arabella said. 'Not that it would matter to me.'

Arabella reached her hand towards Blue Sky's face, prodding the scars she spoke of. Under any other circumstances Blue Sky would not have permitted a woman he barely knew to touch him this way unless he had intentions to bed her. But he considered that Little Sun might be maddened if he offended her maid. Given his desire to lie with her, it would not serve him to cause insult and thus he remained still while Arabella caressed the mark disease had left behind.

'You know, Mistress 'as spent most of the last couple of days in her bed and hasn't had much need for me.' Arabella leaned towards Blue Sky and repositioned her shawl so the slight curve of her breasts were visible. 'I'm certain she wouldn't miss me if you 'ad need of me.'

'Morning Arabella, Morning Blue Sky,' Little Sun's voice came as if out of nowhere. Blue Sky hopped back a good yard from the maid. 'Everything well out here?' she added. When she saw how close Arabella had been standing to him a knowing little smirk crossed her lips that at once sent hot spears through Blue Sky's blood. She thought he was dallying with Arabella… and showed no sign of dismay. Quite the opposite. The thought amused her. Did she think that he dallied with just anyone? If she cared not what he did, or who with, after their time near the river then perhaps it wasn't worth attempting a seduction after all. It was good that he had learned of this now. She had just saved him a great effort.

'Very well, thank you Miss,' said Arabella, scurrying back to her seat.

'Blue Sky, how fares your father?' asked Gilda. She offered him no special look, no tender glance. If she wanted to forget about the kiss they'd shared, that was fine by Blue Sky. As far as he was concerned the less he had to do with her kind the better.

'He is mending well. The skin is red around the stitches but it is nothing.'

Gilda frowned. 'That might be a worrying sign. It's best I ride out and look for myself.'

'There is no need. I did not bring the travois.'

'I have already arranged to borrow Mr Brownlow's horse in case your father was in need of my counsel,' said Gilda. 'I would rather check the wound to be sure.'

'If the lady wishes to ride three miles north for no reason then that is her business,' Blue Sky said.

'I will saddle her up now,' Gilda said, without so much as blinking. Her tendency to ignore his obvious distaste for her only angered him more. He didn't want her at the village. Even while plotting to seduce her over the last few days, he had never dreamed of taking her there. Great Hawk would never be so ungrateful to turn away a woman who had tried to heal him. He felt indebted to be polite. Blue Sky was determined to feel no such debt to any white person, including Gilda. He had been fooled into thinking she might be tender by the way she had asked about the health of his own father mere minutes after learning of the loss of her own. Given her present manner he now realised she had been playing some silly game with him that night. Toying with him for sport or perhaps even plotting to use their intimacy to manipulate him at some future point in time.

He would not allow that to happen.

Arabella stared hungrily at Blue Sky until the clip of horse hooves drew his attention to the end of the row. Gilda sat atop the same steed she had ridden to the James River on a few nights ago. This time, as it was daylight and others would see her, she had mounted the horse side-saddle. She wore a dress of dark navy that clinched her ample curves and her blonde plaited hair hung to one side. Though most of her hair was covered with a white cap, the winding of the braid revealed a slender neck that Blue Sky could easily imagine wrapping his hands around; holding her just where he wanted while he took her for as long as it pleased him. He turned away from her in the hope of banishing the thought.

'Bella,' Gilda called over her shoulder, 'I shouldn't be gone more than a few hours depending on how Great Hawk is feeling. Make yourself useful to Widow Westerby while I'm gone, will you?'

Arabella nodded but as she didn't move from her seat Blue Sky suspected the idle woman would sit there all day while her elder did all the work about the house. He untethered his horse and leapt astride its bare back.

'Try and keep up,' he snapped at Gilda.

'Give me a chance and you'll find I can ride just as hard and fast as you can,' Gilda said with an unmistakable sparkle in her eyes.

A thousand torrid images flashed into Blue Sky's mind at her words and were he not so busy trying to blink them away he might have offered some wry retort. Instead, he glowered. She clearly saw him as entertainment and he didn't take kindly to that idea. He had heard of his kin being shipped to England where white people would pay just to look at the curiosity of their unfamiliar dress and stature. He was not here for her amusement or anyone else's.

When it became clear he was not going to speak, the brightness in Gilda's eyes dimmed but she quickly recovered herself and tapped the horse's side with her foot, spurring the beast into a trot.

Tugging gently at the bridle, Blue Sky maintained his stony expression and rode off after her. Silently, he thanked the Great Spirit that

Gilda Griffiths would soon be gone from Virginia and that this was the last time he would ever have to look upon her. Even as he did so however a sudden ache struck deep in his chest. It was an ache that, over the course of their journey to the village, only became harder to ignore.

# CHAPTER SEVEN

am grateful to you, Little Sun,' Great Hawk said, as Gilda smoothed the last of the chamomile ointment onto the old man's wounds. The native chief sat on a bench, covered with soft bear furs, that ran all around the circumference of the wigwam. At the centre of the domed dwelling, a circle of hot coals smouldered and warmed the atmosphere. If he rested, Great Hawk would heal just fine in this environment.

As Arabella was not with her, one of the village men, who went by the name of Fast River, had assisted Gilda. He was shorter than Blue Sky and had a tranquillity to his deep brown eyes that Blue Sky's lacked.

'It's my deep pleasure to help you,' Gilda said with a smile. She valued kindness above all else and Great Hawk was brimming with it.

'I am sorry about my son's earlier behaviour.'

Gilda shrugged, trying not to think about how briskly Blue Sky had stalked off after they had arrived. Perhaps she should have expected it given that he hadn't said a word to her all the way here. She had thought of little else but seeing him again since they had last parted and when they finally had a chance to engage with each other alone he had remained silent and detached. Even when she had tried to prompt him into conversation she received nothing more than a stiff nod in return.

Though she took pains not to show it, she had found his coolness concerning. 'Something tells me I haven't made the best of impressions on him.'

'It is not you, Little Sun,' Great Hawk said as Gilda lifted his feet up onto the bench, allowing him to lay back and relax. He looked at Fast River then and uttered something in his native tongue that Gilda couldn't understand. Fast River nodded and hurried out of the wigwam.

'I hope you are right – about Blue Sky,' said Gilda. 'I would not wish to cause offence.'

'The fault is not yours,' Great Hawk said. 'Blue Sky has a hatred for white people.'

'Because they are claiming your lands as their own?' Gilda said. Great Hawk was too good-hearted to mention this himself but a person didn't need to be a political mastermind to see what was happening out here.

Great Hawk's long, grey hair swished as he shook his head. 'The Iroquois exiled us from our true homelands long before the white settler came. Though we cannot deny we would prefer to be living peacefully by ourselves, Blue Sky's vendetta is more personal.'

Gilda rubbed her arms, feeling cold all of a sudden despite the warming coals. 'My people did something to Blue Sky specifically?'

'To us both,' Great Hawk said, his wrinkled face sagging. 'They killed Charlotte, Blue Sky's mother, just before his tenth birthday. A new wave of settlers came to Virginia around that time and they did not approve of a white woman bearing me a son.'

Glida's breath caught in her throat. Shame and grief stabbed straight through her. Losing one parent to disease was heart breaking enough, but to lose your mother at the hands of murderers – was that a pain you could ever recover from? No wonder Blue Sky had seemed hostile. Considering this revelation he had been a lot more cordial than he had any need to be.

'I am so terribly sorry,' Gilda said, not knowing what else she could say.

'Not saving Charlotte from the hands of her kin has been my life's biggest regret,' said Great Hawk. 'I lost the woman I love, and I lost my son.'

'Forgive me, I do not follow,' Gilda said, narrowing her eyes. 'Did you have another son? Besides Blue Sky?'

Great Hawk shook his head. 'I lost Blue Sky to anger and revenge. Since the loss of his mother he has pushed everyone away, myself included. His hatred was never quite power-ful enough to make him hate the white woman who gave him life, but he is at war with his white blood. I would never permit him to kill a white man unprovoked but if he believes a white man has wronged him he will stop at nothing to make them pay. Mr Lawson would do well to watch his back right now.'

So that's what Mr Clarke had meant when he said Blue Sky had a reputation. Gilda couldn't out right blame Blue Sky for wanting justice for Lawson's cruelty, he wasn't going to see it in the town court after all, but she had dealt with men like Lawson before. Like rats, they had a way of surviving any threat. What would become of Blue Sky if he tried to take revenge and Lawson got the better of him? An image of Blue Sky's limp body swinging from a noose flashed in her mind and the agony of it almost knocked her off her feet.

She took a deep breath to steady herself and then turned her attentions back to the old man. '*You* did not lose them, Great Hawk. They were taken from you. Your wife in body and your son in soul. My people are the cause of your grief.'

'I know what you say is true,' Great Hawk said, his eyes becoming watery. 'But some days I feel it was my failure.'

Gilda placed a hand on Great Hawk's shoulder and squeezed. 'You must listen to me now. It is not your fault. It has been five years since my mother died from smallpox. My father is a physician and tried everything he could to save her. I felt his pain in my own blood when he couldn't. I cannot pretend this experience compares to yours but I have seen what happens when we blame ourselves for the passing of another. The person we have lost would not want us to feel that way.'

'Perhaps someday I will learn to accept that.'

Gilda sucked in a deep breath. What was happening to Blue Sky's people was wrong and she knew in her heart no small act of healing could close the wound. 'I am sorry for all that happened to you because of us.'

Great Hawk was silent for a moment before responding. 'It wasn't you. The problem is, Blue Sky cannot see a difference between one white person and another.'

'It is a great shame,' Gilda said, trying not to let the disappointment sound out in her tone. The grief she had felt for the passing of her father had clearly granted her a brief reprieve from his hatred, but nothing more.

Still, what was the harm in trying to help him see that not all white people were the enemy? Moreover, if he was still angry with her for her conduct five nights prior she needed to apologise. He had suffered more than enough indignity at the hands of white people without her adding to it further.

'Will you be able to rest for a while?' Gilda asked.

'Oh yes, resting is a wonderful talent of mine,' said Great Hawk.

Gilda chuckled and thanked God for the man's good humour.

'I am pleased to hear it,' she said. 'Before I leave, I need to give Blue Sky instructions on how to care for you after I leave Virginia. Do you know where I might find him?'

'If you walk a mile west of here there is a stream he favours when he is not hunting. I cannot promise he will be there but it is where I would expect him to be.'

Gilda thanked Great Hawk and promised to return for her medicine bag once she had spoken with his son.

As Great Hawk instructed, Gilda set out on foot west of the Indian village and spent the next mile breathing in the fresh, dewy breeze. While she walked, she sighed at the yellow and green expanse of the Virginia plains. In the initial stretch she saw a few other natives of the village. She nodded as she passed and used the greeting 'Bezon' Great Hawk had taught her, much to Blue Sky's distaste, when she had arrived an hour or so ago. Not long after that, Blue Sky had taken his leave without excuse or reason. A native woman holding the tiniest baby she had seen in some time nodded at Gilda and smiled. 'Bezon,' the woman repeated.

After a short while, the only company Gilda had was the soil, the sky and the odd bison grazing lazily in the afternoon sun. She soon spied the stream Great Hawk had described. The water looked so clear and inviting that

Gilda rushed to kneel at the banks; splashing her face before looking further upstream in search of Blue Sky.

She could just make out a figure lying in the long grasses a little way ahead which she presumed to be him. Pushing back up onto her feet, some instinct told her to slow as she approached and without exactly knowing why she tucked herself behind a nearby tree. Peeking out from behind her shelter she was at once glad she had been cautious and not taken Blue Sky by surprise. He lay stretched out in the grasses in the middle of what might best be described an intimate moment. Looking at his bared chest, she remembered how soft his bronzed skin had been to the touch. Just as he had been the first two times they had met, Blue Sky was clad in tight buckskins. What most caught Gilda's attention however was that he had loosened his scarlet breechcloth. At this detail alone, a wetness gathered between her thighs.

Involuntarily, she ran her tongue over her lips as she watched how tightly he gripped his pole; his hips thrusted up towards the clouds as he stroked the length of it. For a moment she was utterly mesmerised and could do nothing but stand and watch the way his big, firm hands moved up and down in a steady, deliberate rhythm. After a few moments his stroking picked up pace and Gilda's breath quickened as she heard the most delicious groan escape his lips.

'Little Sun,' he moaned in his deep, rich voice. 'Little Sun.' Over and over in time to every stroke of his rod.

Gilda gasped, not quite sure of what to do next. She couldn't very well interrupt what Blue Sky was doing. The man would be mortified, not that he had any reason to be. Her hands had wandered the valleys and peaks of her own body more than once in the last four days while thinking of him. His rapture was so enthralling that she very much wished she could simply walk over and replace his hands with her own; to know the power of controlling his every breath and sigh. And what if his fingers found their mark between her thighs too? Her body arched at that thought but she had to push such ideas from her mind.

He would doubtless interpret such advances as an attempt to humiliate rather than pleasure him. He may not have chosen a particularly sheltered place to indulge himself but the Shawnee were, it seemed, more open with their bodies than the settlers. For the sake of Blue Sky's modesty she would hide behind the tree until he had… finished. As Gilda stepped back however she trod on a dry twig that snapped beneath her boots.

In panic, she whipped behind the tree trunk and pressed her back hard against it, her heart pounding, her breath uneven as she prayed to God, and all the saints, that Blue Sky hadn't heard.

# CHAPTER EIGHT

Blue Sky was on the cusp of the most divine fulfilment when he heard a twig snap nearby. Instincts told him it was neither cottontail nor starling and given what he was up to he couldn't very well take the risk of being caught off guard. Whipping to his feet, he cursed under his breath, re-tied his breechcloth and tried to ignore the agonizing throb he felt after being denied that wild peak. Given her smug behaviour back at the yellow house this morning, Blue Sky had thought he could control himself when it came to his desire to bed Gilda Griffiths. Watching her body bounce, arch and flex all the way through the ride to his village however er had proven more temptation than he could take.

The moment he was upright he scanned his surroundings, looking for signs of a possible assailant. The air was still and the lands quiet but there was no mistaking the sound he had heard. It had been close. Since he had come of age and trained to be a brave, he had never once been caught unprepared by his enemy. He was not about to start now. Perhaps someone was lying low in the long grasses? Or behind a longleaf pine?

Easing a small knife from his belt he edged toward the nearest tree, holding his breath as he inched closer. He was but three paces away when he spotted a stretch of navy cloth billowing near the tree roots. It was the same colour as the dress Gilda had been wearing, and was indeed, he concluded, her skirt.

So now the woman was spying on him? Despite all her pretences she really was treacherous at heart. He would have the truth about her agenda this time, and no mistake. A moment later he rounded on the tree, knife in hand. Gilda jumped at the sight of him closing in and he was pleased for it. One day she might spy on the wrong person and live to regret it. Better she learned the lesson from him.

He placed his free hand against the tree so he could lean over her. He would never brandish a knife at a woman but he held his weapon firmly in the other hand, keeping it visible, if only in the background. He wanted to make it clear that she was not going anywhere until he knew her purpose.

'What are you doing here?' he growled. 'Why were you watching me?'

Gilda shook her head. 'I wasn't… I mean, that was not my intent.' Her face was flushed and she bit her lip, her gaze dropped momentarily to Blue Sky's breechcloth and then flitted back up to his eyes.

So, she had liked what she had seen. Though Blue Sky wagered she had got more than she bargained for when she decided to spy on him.

Seeing her again so soon after he had imagined ripping off her clothes sent a raw pulse straight through him but he mustn't let his craving for her body distract from the truth of what she was: just another deceitful settler.

'Don't lie to me,' he barked. 'Tell me why you are here.'

'That tone will get you no answers,' Gilda said, raising her chin.

Blue Sky noticed once more the inexplicable fire in her turquoise eyes. She had courage, he would give her that. He lowered his voice just enough to appear civil.

'Have I not the right to be angry when I find you sneaking around my lands?'

'I wasn't sneaking anywhere. I came to find out if you were angry with me for what passed between us the other night,' said Gilda. She had recovered from the embarrassment of being caught and her distaste for his previous tone. Her voice had returned to its usual gentle manner.

'Why would I be angry about that?' Blue Sky said, forcing himself to keep some of the snap in his voice.

'From your manner it seemed you felt I had overstepped. If that is the case, even though I was in grief at the time, I wanted to apologise... again.'

'I am not angry about that.'

'Oh.' Gilda frowned. He watched her eyes fill with confusion. It looked to be genuine, but how could you tell with her kind?

'Then, may I ask what I have done to displease you in the last four days without having seen or heard from you?'

'Nothing.'

Her eyebrows arched. 'Nothing?'

'That's what I said.'

'I see,' said Gilda. 'If that is the case, I shall not waste another moment of your time.' She made an attempt to duck under his arm but he blocked her. She stared at him, her gaze unwavering. Most women of the town would be unnerved by this whole exchange and start begging him not to hurt them, assuming because his skin was darker than theirs that he would mistreat a lady. But Gilda showed no signs of either fear or distress.

'Blue Sky,' she said, her voice softening further. 'If you tell me why you are angry, I might be able to repair whatever damage I've done,' she said. An innocent look surfaced in her eyes that made him want to close any distance between them at once. 'Won't you at least give me the opportunity?' she pushed.

Blue Sky glowered but try as he might he could not deny her an answer. 'You thought I was dallying with Arabella this morning.'

'Did I?' Gilda said. 'How interesting. What else did I think this morning?'

'Nothing. You did not care if I was trifling with her.'

'And this angered you?'

'Yes.'

'Because… you wanted me to care if you were trifling with Bella?'

Blue Sky couldn't muster a verbal response this time. It was too humiliating. But he offered her a vague nod.

A pained look crossed her face as she reached a hand to his cheek. His first instinct was to pull away but he could not make himself. He… didn't want to. He wanted her hands on him. 'I did not think you were being intimate with Bella.'

'I told you not to lie to me.'

She dropped her hand and he at once regretted his words but it could not be denied: she was trying to deceive him and he wouldn't take it.

'You have spent little more than an hour with me all told and you expect to be able to read my innermost thoughts?' said Gilda.

'I know what I saw,' he said, but even he could hear the uncertainty in his voice.

'Not that I owe you explanation, but the look on my face was one of mild amusement at Bella attempting to get your attention when you didn't appear interested.'

Could that be true? Gilda had smirked, and he had thought her amused... A feeling of foolishness washed over Blue Sky, and yet he was still not satisfied by her answer.

'But you would not care if I was trying to lie with her?'

Gilda drew a deep breath, one that made her breasts swell so high that he almost forgot he had asked her a question.

'Blue Sky, I kissed you, uninvited, and I will be gone from Virginia in ten sunsets. What right do I have to make any claim on you? To judge your behaviour or stop you pursuing whomever you wish to pursue?'

While Blue Sky admired the free-spirited manner by which she had judged the situation he swallowed hard at the mention of her leaving. He turned for a moment to sheath his knife in a bid to conceal the strange aching he felt at that thought.

'But,' she added. 'If I am completely truthful, I would care if you tried to lie with Bella.'

Blue Sky turned back to her and those wide, beseeching eyes that seemed to penetrate the armour he had spent years constructing to keep all he knew at a distance. It was better that way. He would never have to suffer again like he did when his mother was killed. And yet, as he looked into Gilda's freckled face protecting himself felt less important, less necessary. For no reason he could fathom, he would rather be protecting her. 'Truly? You would care if I was with someone else? Even though, as you say, we are strangers.'

Gilda nodded. 'I never expected it to mean anything to you. But the kiss we shared, well, it was the most passionate and magical moment I have ever experienced.'

'Is that so?' Blue Sky said. He was smiling before he could stop himself.

'Yes,' she said. 'The only reasons I held back from taking matters further that night is that I was afraid I was putting you in an unfair position where you felt you couldn't deny me because of my grief. And...'

'And what? Tell me.' Blue Sky said, as a thousand possible reasons for her rejection swarmed in his mind.

'The last man I was with... it didn't end favourably.'

At the mention of another man, Blue Sky's chest tightened a notch. But Gilda was hardly his first woman so it didn't seem fair to judge her differently than he did himself. Better to focus on her other words. What did she mean that it didn't end favourably? Had some brute hurt this tender woman? If so, she had been far too forgiving of his behaviour since they had met.

And what about the revelation that she had not wanted their time together to end five nights ago? Or that he stirred excitement in her? A fact she had admitted freely and honestly. He could barely look her in the eye as the shame hit him. He had plotted to callously seduce and abandon a good woman. But, could it really be classed as abandonment when she was the one leaving? Blue Sky couldn't get that part straight in his mind. The one truth that penetrated was that she wanted him. She wanted him as he wanted her. Opportunities such as this were not made to be squandered.

'Kissing me is your most passionate and magical moment…?' Blue Sky said, his face drifting closer to hers.

Gilda took a deep sigh before whispering: 'My most passionate and magical moment ever.'

'Until now,' Blue Sky said, closing the gap between her mouth and his and delivering a deep, hard kiss.

# CHAPTER NINE

Gilda smouldered at the unexpected force of Blue Sky's lips as they traced a trail from her mouth across her cheek bone and over to her ear.

'I want you, Little Sun. I've wanted you since the moment I saw you,' he murmured.

The mere rush of his breath against her ear was enough to draw a sigh from her, let alone the words it carried. He truly desired her. Not out of pity or politeness but because of the same raw want she felt for him. And *Little Sun*, the way he pronounced that name left her weak.

'Blue Sky,' she whispered, pulling back just far enough to touch her nose against the side of his. 'I don't understand it, but... I've never wanted anyone more than I do you... right now.'

She watched his pupils dilate with what looked to her like uncontrollable lust. He ripped away her cap and the next thing she felt were his fingers lacing into her hair where it met the back of her neck. He then tugged on her blonde locks, loosening her plait in a manner that at once ignited a thousand tiny sparks along every nerve in her body. She didn't miss the chance to run her fingers through his long, dark hair either; its silky quality intensified her already frantic need for him. After everything she had been through, she shouldn't want this. She shouldn't want anyone. And yet as Blue Sky caressed and squeezed her every curve, she was sure she had craved his roughened hands on her even before they had met.

She returned his kisses in any place her lips could reach him: his forehead, his nose, his ear, his chin but then, remembering what she had witnessed just a short time earlier, she charted a more deliberate path down the centre of his chest all the way to his navel; revelling in the saltiness of his soft, bronzed skin until she was on her knees in front of him.

Slowly, as though Gilda were a woodland elk he might scare with any sudden movement, Blue Sky began to untie his breechcloth.

As he did so, she looked up at those ocean deep eyes and could hardly believe what she heard herself say next.

'Please, Blue Sky. Please, do not deny me. I need to feel you... in my mouth.'

An almost pained expression crossed his face at her words. His movements quickened then and the deep red material fell to the ground, revealing his hardened shaft.

The mere sight left Gilda breathless and panting as she took in the view of him standing there in nothing but his buckskins. Her heart was beating faster than she remembered it ever beating before. Why had she said that she wanted him in her mouth? She did want that, there was no denying it, but she didn't have any experience in pleasing a man that way. Still, as she studied his firm, muscular form she realised it was impossible to look at a body like Blue Sky's and not get any ideas about where she might start.

Running her tongue over her lips to moistening them, she leaned towards him and kissed just the tip of his manhood while staring up into his eyes. At this gesture, Blue Sky made the most luscious groan. His face took on that pained look again, making it clear that he was aching for this just as much as she was. Spurred on by his obvious desire, she slowly began kissing her way down his thickened rod. She worked her mouth around it from every angle she could find and did not overlook the soft, tight sacks hanging between his thighs. The more she flicked and rubbed her tongue against him, the lounder he groaned and she relished the sound so much, she thought she might spend forever making sure every inch had been properly, thoroughly kissed.

The thought of him burying himself deep in her mouth however, and the pleasure that might bring him, was too tempting a prospect to ignore for long. She never knew it was possible for a woman to ache for something like that, the way she ached right now. Thus, after several minutes of listening to his heart-quickening moans, she positioned her tongue beneath his pole and slowly licked her way along the length from base to tip. She held just the top of him between her lips then, massaging the smooth skin with her tongue, until Blue Sky could bear the tease no longer and thrust his hips forward, driving himself into her wet, warm mouth.

Gilda luxuriated in his heat and the sense of him filling a once-empty space left her needing more. She opened her mouth wider to show how hungry she was to please, welcoming his charge as he pushed deeper. His growls became more ferocious by the second and he began to stroke her hair as she slowly, steadily bobbed her head up and down.

'Your mouth is perfect... perfect. Please don't stop,' Blue Sky gasped, pushing beyond her mouth now and into her throat.

Had her mouth not been otherwise occupied, Gilda would have smiled demurely at Blue Sky's words. Stopping, or easing up in any way, was the furthest thing from her mind. She was transfixed by his every sound and movement. The tender ferocity of his thrusts was driving her wild with want and all the while his hands pulled at her hair with increasing force, and desperation.

She began grazing his inner thighs with her fingernails and then reached up to gently caress the tight sacks between them. At this, Blue Sky shivered with renewed excitement. His pace quickened and she could feel by the trembling in his legs that he was riding the cliff edge of ecstasy. Wanting nothing more than to send him over that euphoric precipice, Gilda grabbed Blue Sky's bared buttocks and pulled him against her so that her head was pinned hard against the tree trunk. She moaned over the length of him, listening to his ragged breath, digging her nails into his skin, deeper and deeper, until he ground against her with all of his considerable might. Mere moments later she felt him reach that brutal pinnacle as he cried out his name for her: 'Little Sun...' over and over, and his hot seed shot down her throat.

# CHAPTER TEN

lue Sky pulled Gilda into the long grasses and rolled himself on top of her.

'Why are you so perfect?' he whispered, before kissing her precious forehead, and those full, sumptuous lips that just moments ago had feasted on him with a dedication, the likes of which he had never seen from other women he had bedded. She looked up at him as if he were the Great Spirit himself. Her eyelids looked heavy and dreamy as she ran her fingers through his hair.

What was happening to him? He was sure that taking this woman once would be enough, just as it had been with all of the others. But the pleasure he had taken in Little Sun somehow only made him crave her more. He would never forget the delightful gagging sound she had made just as he reached his peak, nor the sight of her so willingly swallowing down his seed. And the way she had begged for him. *Begged.* Without his asking; without any games, or instruction. She had wanted him. Wanted to please him, and, oh, how she had. He was breathless from all the ways she had made him feel alive.

If she had any notion that their encounter was drawing to a close however, she was very much mistaken. After all she had given him, freely and without a thought to her own satisfaction, he wanted nothing more than to watch those full lips form the perfect O. He imagined her ravishing moans to be nothing short of musical but there was only one way know for sure.

He had paused merely to manoeuvre her into a more sheltered position. Being caught had been the furthest thing from his mind when she had knelt before him and stared up with those big blue eyes, but he would need to be more careful for the sake of her reputation. It was much less likely they would be spotted in the grasses. There, they would lie too low for anyone scanning the land to see them.

After his somewhat forceful taking of her mouth he wanted to reassure her of his tenderness and thus began to slowly work his tongue against hers. She responded at once, wrapping her arms tight around him.

'Blue Sky,' she whispered, tangling her fingers in his hair. 'You are the one who is perfect.'

At these words, a wide smile, that he could not stop and did not even try to, spread across his lips. He could not remember ever feeling as secure and warm inside as he did just now. He had no doubt she was the cause and for that she deserved to receive the same in kind.

Slowly, he began to kiss her neck before moving his lips downward to her chest. In one sharp movement, he tore at her corset and gained just enough slack to bare her breasts so that they perched, two, creamy jutting orbs, above the neckline of her dress. Blue Sky held them with both hands, marvelling at how soft her skin was. Delaying no further, he pushed the rounds together so he need turn his head only a touch in either direction for his tongue to find its mark. Little Sun's body rippled beneath him as he sucked each of her nipples in turn. The taste and smell of her was intoxicating: a blend of salt, rosewater and lemon. He wondered if he could ever get enough and it seemed she felt much the same about his caresses. Her body arched harder towards him as he continued to work his tongue over her breasts and her moaning was so loud he was sure someone from the village would hear them a mile from where they lay. Blue Sky wished he could have cared more that they might be heard but in truth her passionate sighs only spurred him on to bring her deeper pleasure and draw even louder moans from that faultless little mouth.

He slipped his hands under her petticoats and slowly drew them up to her waist, revealing a pair of curvaceous legs part-concealed by her ribboned stockings. The view was even more tempting than he had imagined and he wasted not a minute in hooking her knees over his shoulders.

'Oh, Blue Sky,' Little Sun whispered, as he leant down and took his first taste of her. He couldn't believe how aroused she was; he had never known a woman be so ready to receive him. It seemed she had enjoyed him taking her mouth almost as much as he had. At that thought, though he would have thought it impossible, Blue Sky began to feel himself stiffening once more. Unable to contain his longing, he began to lick low and hard between her thighs. Little Sun at once thrust her hips towards his tongue, allowing him deeper access. He moaned long enough and loud enough for her to know that he thought the taste of her exquisite. Her nectar was both sweet and salty, a tantalizing combination. Reaching his hands up to squeeze her breasts, he licked through the soft down, breaking through to her most sensitive spot.

Little Sun writhed her body against his face for some time, pushing herself harder into him as each moment passed. He had moved his tongue lower and lower until he seemed to have discovered some unmarked sweet spot that reduced her to complete abandon. As soon as he found this mark, he focused all of his efforts on that one point and watched with nothing short of wonder as her eyes rolled back in her head. He delivered a pleasure so intense, by her expression, it seemed she was attached to this world by a mere thread.

The first sign of her climax was the shaking of her thighs. Slight at first but then it spread to her knees and her arms. Blue Sky increased the speed and depth at which he pushed his tongue inside her. His renewed enthusiasm was more than she could stand. In a matter of moments she began to whimper and her whole body, her whole being it seemed, shook wildly as she reached that delicious moment of violent bliss.

## CHAPTER ELEVEN

Gilda was grateful to Blue Sky for giving her a private moment or two to rearrange her stay into its original position in case they were caught off guard by a passer-by. The moment she was satisfied with her presentation however, he took her in his arms and lay with her against the base of the tree he'd found her hiding behind what now seemed forever ago.

She needed no invitation to wrap her arms around him before letting out a satisfied sigh. Gilda had had mixed sexual encounters back in England. One that might best be described as cordial and several others with the same suitor that were so filled with cruelty that she tried not to think about them. Neither man had lain with her afterwards or held her against their body as though she was treasured, the way Blue Sky did now. As such, sexual intimacy was, historically, rarely a topic on her mind. She was at her most comfortable sifting through medical volumes and keeping her thoughts on more productive avenues. After her experience this afternoon however, she had a feeling that would change.

'Can I ask you something?' Blue Sky said, tracing his finger around the palm of her hand. His merest touch sent goosebumps racing across her skin. Why did this man affect her so? His general manner towards her had been aloof at best. That would not usually draw her in. Had some part of her sensed the bewildering tenderness and passion he had shown in the past hour? Had she somehow known there was a doting soul behind all that armour?

Gilda stroked the side of his face with the scar on it, trying to memorise the unfamiliar indentations and crests using just her fingertips. 'I think we're rather past idle pleasantries, you may ask me anything you wish.'

'Good,' he said, running a hand through her hair. 'Why – why did you help my father, back in the market square?'

Gilda sighed. She wished Blue Sky lived in a world where there was no need to ask such a question. One in which it was just obvious that you would help a fellow who was wounded, regardless of the colour of his skin.

'My grandfather visited Jamestown many years ago, not long after the first settlers came,' she explained. 'While he was there he sent my father a number of letters. They weren't for my eyes but I am... naturally inquisitive and read them anyway. They told of much senseless brutality and cruel trickery to the natives who lived on this side of the ocean.'

Blue Sky was silent for a moment before speaking. 'You know then, what your people have done to mine.'

Gilda nodded. 'They weren't supposed to, you know. Even now the official line in England is to be friendly with the natives who live here.'

Blue Sky shook his head. 'That is not my experience.'

'I know,' said Gilda. 'I knew even before I met you. I remember crying the first time I read those letters. I reread them again before I ventured here. The contents kept me awake almost every night of the voyage.'

'So, you helped us because you felt guilty?'

'Yes. But also because, even though the wrongs of the past cannot be undone, that doesn't mean I shouldn't try and set an example about how your people should be treated in the future.'

Blue Sky held her tighter, and she leaned over to kiss the tribal motif inked along his arms, dark chevrons pointing upwards towards the sky, after which he was named.

'I am sorry for the loss of your father,' said Blue Sky. 'Arabella said you had spent much of the time we've been apart in your bed.'

'Yes. I needed time… I haven't told her or Widow Westerby about my father's passing. I couldn't face the questions I don't have answers to.'

'What questions?' Blue Sky said, a frown passing over his face.

'There is something... odd about him dying so suddenly. Andrew, my brother, said he seemed to have passed in his sleep but he was too young for that and was very healthy.' A thought too terrible to verbalise or even fully acknowledge skittered across Gilda's mind. The man she had fled once said that her family would pay the price if she ever left him. But surely he wouldn't carry out that threat if he thought her dead?

'Sometimes people die, and we don't know why,' Blue Sky said, breaking through Gilda's thoughts. 'If your father died in his sleep it was a peaceful passing.'

'I'm grateful for that at least,' Gilda said, trying not to let the pain she still felt at being orphaned sound out in her voice while being almost certain that she had failed. This was confirmed when Blue Sky kissed the top of her head; she couldn't hide her grief from him.

'Did your companions not wonder why you slept so long?'

'Bella did,' Gilda said with a smile. 'She is nothing if not curious. But I told her that I just needed rest after the voyage. I will write to Andrew and hopefully he will send more news when I arrive in New Orleans.'

'I have heard of that place. The French city far to the south. That is where you intend to go?'

Was that sadness in Blue Sky's voice at the mention of her leaving? It sounded as such and he had seemed hurt when he thought she didn't care if he was dallying with Arabella. Still, Gilda doubted he could have become attached to her after one encounter and even if she did have feelings for him that she had experienced for no other, it was too dangerous to indulge them. The lateness of her ship had cost them enough time already. As soon as she and Arabella had properly rested they must leave Williamsburg at once.

'Yes, New Orleans is our planned destination but, much like my father's passing, you're the only person who knows that. I haven't even told Bella where I'm planning on taking us. Can you be trusted with these secrets, I wonder?' Gilda flashed Blue Sky a smile. His face however remained serious and an uneasy silence fell between them.

'Why does everything you do have to be a secret?'

She reached a hand up and turned his chin to her. 'I know it seems suspicious. But can you trust me if I tell you that I have my reasons and they are for both our safety?'

Blue Sky nodded but pulled his face away from her touch.

This pained her more than she could have imagined but telling him any more could put him in great jeopardy. If he hated her for being guarded she would have to let him. The tender ruggedness of this man was beguiling but she could not get involved. If her darkest suspicions about her father's death were true then it meant *he* might know that she was still alive. In which case, she had no choice but to put as much distance as she could between herself and *him*. Even if it meant leaving behind a lover she would never forget.

She frowned, noticing, beyond Blue Sky's perfect face, the position of the sun. It was already starting to sink in the west. How long had they laid here? It had felt like mere moments. 'I should go,' she said, trying to ignore the churn in her stomach at the thought of leaving him.

He stood and tied his hair into a knot atop his head. 'I will ride back to town with you. It is right and honourable to make sure you are safely returned to your people.'

'Thank you,' she said, while wishing he hadn't made the task sound quite so official. It seemed their time together that afternoon was destined to be nothing more than a brief dalliance; a mere memory to warm her on more than a hundred long and lonely nights that awaited between Virginia and New Orleans.

## CHAPTER TWELVE

The sun had almost set when Blue Sky and Gilda's steeds trotted back into Queen Street. It was at once clear that there would be no final, stolen kisses before they parted. Blue Sky's eyes narrowed as he examined the small crowd of Williamsburg townsmen, including Clarke and Lawson, who stood around the porch of the yellow house, talking with Arabella and Widow Westerby. His stomach clenched. Anything involving Lawson could only mean trouble.

'Thank the Lord and Jesus,' Widow Westerby said as they dismounted their horses.

'I'm so pleased you ain't 'urt, Miss,' Arabella chimed in.

Gilda frowned and walked towards the small gathering. 'Why would I be hurt? What's going on?'

'We was just about to ride out to the village and check they hadn't skinned you alive,' Lawson said.

Gilda shook her head. 'Forgive me, I am still at a loss as to what is going on here.'

'Please Miss,' said Arabella. 'You've been gone a lot longer than we expected. Mr Lawson came to call and when I told 'im where you were and how long you'd been gone, he started to worry. He fetched Mr Clarke and they were going to ride out and find you.'

At this, Blue Sky was sorely tempted to turn his back on them and ride away but, even if she had her secrets and planned on deserting him, he could not leave Gilda to fend for herself after the time they had spent together. He scowled at Lawson who, he knew, would have taken any excuse to ride out on his village and maybe kill a few of his kin into the bargain when Clarke wasn't looking. Glancing at Gilda out of the corner of his eye, he cursed himself. He had kept her in his arms too long and aroused suspicion, and yet it had been nowhere near long enough.

'While I appreciate the concern,' Gilda said, in a tone that made it clear she didn't appreciate their concern at all, 'I was in no need of rescuing.'

'Then what was you doing out there all these hours, huh?' Lawson sneered.

'Funny that you should be the one to ask that question Mr Lawson,' said Gilda. 'If it weren't for you I wouldn't have to spend any time at all in Blue Sky's village. They could have some peace from us whites.'

At Gilda's words, Lawson's face turned purple. 'You mean we're supposed to believe you been fixing a scratch on some old savage all these hours?'

'You may believe what you wish,' Gilda said.

'Huh.' Lawson spat. The splash on the dusty ground landed not far from Gilda's skirt. 'You ask me, she been tumbling with the half-breed.'

At this Blue Sky took three deliberate steps towards Lawson. He wasn't going to stand by and watch him intimidate Gilda. And frankly, if the fool was going to give him an excuse to wipe that smug leer off his face once and for all, then he would surely take it.

'Easy now Blue Sky,' said Clarke. 'We don't want no trouble here. The lady's safe and was clearly with you of her own accord. That's good enough for me.'

Blue Sky glowered at Clarke. The magistrate should have dealt with Lawson after he stabbed Great Hawk. Now, because there had been no repercussions for knifing a native man, Lawson knew he could get away with whatever he wished. Someone had to teach him that there were some lines you didn't cross.

Gilda stepped forward to where Blue Sky was standing and put a hand on his arm. 'Blue Sky, I'll handle it.'

At this, he folded his arms across his chest and did all he could to avoid visibly softening at her touch.

'How dare you throw around such filthy slanders Mr Lawson?' Gilda said. 'I don't know exactly what your quarrel is with me, when just the other day I was tending your wounds, but I would ask you not to casual-

ly cast such heinous doubt on my modesty.'
Gilda's face contorted in such disgust as she
spoke that Blue Sky could barely contain his
pain.

So that's how she really felt when it came
down to it? Lawson's filthy slanders of her trifling with a filthy Indian repulsed her? He understood the need for her to protect her reputation but the expression on her face told him
it was more than that. She was ashamed of
him and what they had done together. That's
why, no matter what pleasure they had giv-
en each other, she wouldn't stay. Why did he
ever deceive himself into expecting more from
her? If that was how she felt, he would not
spoil her good reputation any further.

'I would never stoop to bedding one of
your kind, Lawson. It would risk lying with a
woman who might be in some way related to
you.' Blue Sky said before turning on his heel
and walking away.

'You dirty little mongrel, I should put a
knife through you too,' Lawson shouted after
him.

Blue Sky stopped and paused for a brief moment, just long enough to leave Lawson wondering what he was going to do to him. Then, pulling the knife from his belt, he lunged towards his foe at speed. Before he knew what was happening however, Gilda had whipped around in front of him and shielded Lawson with her person. 'Blue Sky, no!'

His knife stopped less than an inch from Gilda's heart. She stared at it, pale and breathless, surely understanding the same thing he did: if his reflexes had been slower, even by a whisker, she would have been dead on the ground. He would have killed her. His eyes widened at the thought and hot tears threatened but he held them back with all his might. Lawson would take it as a sign of weakness or would guess he had affections for Gilda - and goodness knows what he might do with her then. He could not let another woman suffer the same fate as his mother on his account.

'Blue Sky!' Clarke barked while Arabella and Widow Westerby gasped and lamented somewhere in the periphery. 'You stand down. So help me, I'm going to have you in the court house for this.'

'Given that Blue Sky was provoked I don't think that's particularly just, Mr Clarke, do you?' said Gilda, still catching her breath.

'He could have killed you,' said Clarke.

'And Lawson could have killed his father.'

'That's different,' Lawson started to pipe up again.

'All right, I've had enough,' Clarke said. 'Blue Sky, you need to go back to the village now, and, if you know what's good for you, you won't show your face in town for a good, long while. The rest of you need to go home. Miss Griffiths is safe, and seemingly doesn't want to take this further, this is all over nothing.'

Blue Sky turned and mounted his horse without looking back, reproaching himself for letting his guard down so easily. Hadn't he learned not to trust the whites by now? He had opened up to just one of them and what had it brought him? Accusations, public humiliation and blatant disgust on Gilda's part. In just a few seconds he was galloping back towards his village. Telling himself that after seeing the obvious revulsion in Gilda's eyes, and given all the trouble that had been waiting for him back in Williamsburg, that the best thing for them both was never to see each other again. No woman, no matter how eager or tender to the touch, was worth this amount of trouble.

# CHAPTER
# THIRTEEN

ilda and Arabella were just bedding down for second sleep, about to blow out their candle, when they were startled by a hard rapping at the front door of Widow Westerby's home. Gilda jumped and her first thought, her only thought, was that *he* had found her.

Arabella frowned across at Gilda from her bed, likely wondering why a knock at the door, even one past midnight, would cause her mistress such alarm. 'Who's that at this hour?' she groaned. 'Suppose I'd better go and see.'

'No,' Gilda said, before her maid could swing her feet out of bed. The last thing she wanted was to find out who was standing behind that door but if it was *him* she couldn't be sure what he might do to Arabella just to get to her.

Slowly, Gilda pulled back the curtain and looked down from the window, trying to catch sight of their late night visitor. But alas, the porch roof shielded them from view.

'I'll see to it,' said Gilda, rising and tying on a silk wrapper. She then turned in such a way that Arabella didn't see her silently ease open the drawer next to her bed. Feeling for the pistol Andrew had given her before she set sail for America. Discreetly, she pocketed the weapon, alongside the pouch full of gunpowder and shots lying next to it.

'What are you doing?' Arabella asked.

'Nothing, just making myself respectable,' Gilda lied. Her maid did not need to know she had been carrying a pistol all this time. It was only a precaution after all. There was very little chance she would need to use it. The person at the door might be anyone.

She knew who she wanted it to be.

The look in Blue Sky's eyes when he had almost driven his knife through her heart yesterday afternoon had nearly killed her when his blade didn't. She at once saw the horror written across his face and with the crowd watching on she had not been able to take him into her arms as she had wanted nor offer him forgiveness for what she understood to be complete accident.

Another rattle at the door, much harder and more urgent this time, wrenched her from her thoughts. Steeling herself, she left the bedroom, securing the door behind her, and stepped out onto the small landing. She had descended only two stairs when she felt a stiff hand on her shoulder.

Crying out, Gilda reeled only to see the anxious face of Widow Westerby.

'No need to worry yourself,' Gilda said, dreading what might happen if the old woman followed her and her worst fears were realised. 'I'll call up if it's somebody asking after you.'

'All right child, but don't open the door to anyone you don't know, now.' Ironic, Gilda thought. Strangers were not what concerned her but someone she knew all too well.

Slowly, she made her way downstairs by candlelight trying to control her shaking. The rapping started again, and again she jumped. If it was *him*, she would settle it quietly. She would tell him that Briar Chatterton no longer existed. That she had died the day she left him the note, explaining that she would rather walk into the River Witham with her pockets full of stones than marry him. If he would not politely accept that the woman who agreed to marry him was long dead, she would use the pistol to persuade him it was in his best interests to walk away. That wouldn't keep her safe forever, she understood. But it would suffice until morning when she could alert Mr Clarke. Pulling the pistol from her pocket, she neared the window and drew the thin curtains back an inch, praying the visitor's eyes were elsewhere as she did so.

Beneath the pale moonlight, she could make out a bearded figure in a finely-cut coat. Her muscles slackened. The silhouette was not broad enough to be his. Whoever it was held a lantern and as he turned further in her direction, she could see it was Mr Clarke.

She dashed to the door at once, only just remembering to pocket the pistol and its accompanying pouch before unlocking the door.

'Mr Clarke, are you well?'

'Pardon the late hour Miss Griffiths. It's my wife. She's about to birth a child. We've been trying to alert the town doctor, Mr Simmonds, for hours and when we finally found him, well he's had a bit too much whisky at the tavern tonight to be delivering my firstborn. Do you have experience?'

'I was trained by my church back in Lincoln. I have delivered several children myself, Sir and assisted my father in delivering many more. Give me just a few moments and I will accompany you. You... haven't left your wife alone have you?'

'No, our maid Elsie is with her.'

Gilda nodded and then scurried upstairs to dress. Arabella was slow to get going, having prepared herself for another four hours of shut-eye, but when Gilda mentioned that she had had little work to occupy her over the last few days, she soon remembered her duties, joining Gilda and Mr Clarke as quickly as she could.

Gilda had no wish to get into pleasantries with Clarke. He had failed to prevent Lawson from stabbing Great Hawk and then failed again to protect her honour when Lawson was throwing slanders yesterday. True enough, Lawson wasn't far wrong in his suspicions about what she and Blue Sky had been up to but it was a rotten thing to say so publicly. Mercifully, Mr Clarke lived rather close to Widow Westerby and it was just a few short minutes before they arrived at his dwelling: a long, white house about half way down England Street.

'Oh Lord,' Arabella said, as they entered the bedroom to find Mrs Clarke in a state of sweaty distress. Elsie lightly dabbed her lady's forehead with a damp cloth but Gilda could tell from her widened eyes that this was the first time their maid had accompanied a woman in labour.

'That will be enough of that kind of comment thank you Bella,' said Gilda. 'Mr Clarke perhaps it would be best for you to be else-where?'

Mr Clarke did not have to be asked twice to leave the room. As soon as they were alone, Gilda held Mrs Clarke's hand and gave it a squeeze. She was much younger than her husband, Gilda would guess by twenty years or so. The woman stared at her new midwife with dark eyes behind a curtain of raven hair.

'Mrs Clarke, how long have you been in labour?'

'It feels like years,' she replied.

'It's maybe been four hours,' Elsie said.

'There's blood...' Mrs Clarke said, nodding to the space between her legs. 'Everywhere...'

'That's to be expected when one is trying to push a whole new person out of them,' Gilda replied.

Mrs Clarke emitted a weary chuckle. 'Oh, do not make me laugh right now.'

'Can't promise that I'm afraid,' Gilda said, with a small, reassuring smile. 'But let me take a closer look and check what baby's up to.' She was just about to start examining the woman when she noticed Arabella and Elsie had started a chit-chat. The pair were giggling as though they were sitting in the park having a picnic.

'Elsie?'

'Yes Ma'am?'

'Try not to let Bella be a bad influence on you in the short time she's here. Some freshly boiled water and some clean cloths will come in handy if you can round them up.'

'Right away, Ma'am,' said Elsie, disappearing to fulfil Gilda's instruction.

'What an obedient maid you have,' Gilda said, moving down to the end of the bed to inspect Mrs Clarke's progress. 'You don't have one going spare, do you?'

'Mistress!' Arabella said, putting her hands on her hips. ''Ow can you say such a thing with me standing right 'ere?'

Gilda raised a knowing eyebrow at Arabella before completing the rest of her examination. The woman's labour was quite advanced. It was lucky Mr Clarke had summoned her when he did. Within just a few minutes Elsie returned with the water and the cloths but after that point it transpired to be a hard night indeed.

Gilda could do little to ease Mrs Clarke's pain and it soon became clear the child was going to come feet first, always a more complicated job. Gilda watched poor Mrs Clarke's face contorting in agony. If Gilda's suspicions about her own body were correct, she would never experience the pain Mrs Clarke suffered then. Though the word of God encouraged her to embrace all of her womanly duties, including rearing children, watching her new patient, she couldn't say she was disappointed to escape this particular responsibility on medical grounds. It was with great relief from all present that just after three o clock a baby boy struggled out into the world.

Once Mrs Clarke and the baby were presentable, they invited Mr Clarke to meet his son.

'Why hello there little fella,' Mr Clarke said, cradling the baby, whom Gilda had wrapped in a blanket. She smiled to herself. People always turned strange when they had a new-born in their hands. She wondered if the undesirables of Williamsburg would still be intimidated by Mr Clarke if they saw him monkey-talking to his son.

'What'll you call him?' Arabella asked.

'We're going to name him after' – Mr Clarke began but Mrs Clarke raised a weary hand to his arm.

'There were some difficult moments there, Charles. If it weren't for Miss Griffiths I don't think either myself or our son would have made it through. She should name the child.'

'Oh no, I couldn't,' said Gilda, waving her hands in alarm. 'I was merely doing my job.'

'No, no,' said Mr Clarke. 'My wife is right, and I insist. He can take my father's name as the middle name. It would be our honour if you would christen our son.'

'If… you insist,' Gilda said, her eyes filling with tears as she realised what the only fitting name for the baby was. 'My father passed on quite recently. His name was Henry.'

'Henry,' said Mr Clarke. 'A fine name.'

'A king's name,' Mrs Clarke added.

'Hello Henry Cuthbert Clarke,' said Mr Clarke.

'Cuthbert?' said Arabella.

'An equally fine name,' Gilda interjected before Arabella could say anything more. 'But forgive me I am tired and must rest. I'm sure you won't mind us leaving you to your new family. I have informed Elsie of her duties in caring for mother and babe, though if you are worried about anything please do call on the Widow Westerby's house at once.'

'We are mighty grateful to you Miss Griffiths,' said Clarke, nodding to her as she took her leave with Arabella in tow.

When they stepped outside, the pink hue to the sky told Gilda the sun would be up before long. Thank goodness the walk back to her bed would be brief.

'Mistress…'

'Yes Bella?'

'I'm sorry to learn about your father.'

'Thank you.'

'And Mistress?'

'Yes Bella,' Gilda said, trying to supress a sigh. She knew her maid meant well but she was exhausted and did not wish to be questioned about painful topics on so little sleep.

'I meant to say I was sorry about what happened yesterday, with Mr Lawson.'

'It's not your fault, Bella. Mr Lawson seems ever to be sporting for a fight.'

'You may be right about that, but 'e was only looking after you Miss. You can't be too careful around them Indians.'

Gilda stopped walking and shot her maid a stern look. 'There's no need to fear the native people here, Bella.'

'Oh yes there is, they're dirty the lot of them. And they're always stealing what's ours.'

'Not too dirty for you to be asserting yourself with Blue Sky yesterday morning,' Gilda said.

'Come on Miss, that's all their kind's good for. 'Avin' a bit of fun with to cheer yourself up. But no more. You don't want to get too close to one of them.'

'How dare you speak about Blue Sky's people that way?' Gilda said, raising her voice louder than she meant to. 'What would you know about them? What time have you spent in their company other than your brief moments tending Great Hawk?'

Arabella fell silent and at least had the decency to look ashamed.

'I think it's best you go on back to the house without me,' said Gilda. 'Here take my bag, will you.'

'I thought you were tired, Miss,' Arabella said in a quiet voice.

'I am,' Gilda said, 'but I am suddenly in need of a walk alone. I'll be home when I'm home. Do not come looking for me. And if Mr Lawson should make any more unwanted visits you can tell him I am tending someone in the town.'

Nodding, and for once realising she had over-stepped, Arabella took Gilda's bag and scurried off in the direction of Queen Street.

Without really thinking about where she was walking, Gilda started towards the square near The Capitol building. Nobody would be there at this time of day and she could take the opportunity to sit and enjoy some precious quiet time, a luxury she had sorely missed since she first stepped on the boat from England.

No sooner had she found a seat for herself upon grass however than she heard a deep voice ask: 'Little Sun, are you hurt?'

# CHAPTER FOURTEEN

'Blue Sky...' Gilda said, raising those big turquoise eyes to him. He almost lost his resolve and kissed her there and then. But he held back. No matter what, he had to hold himself back.

'What are you doing here?'

'Are you hurt?' he repeated, his tone harsher.

'Hurt? No...'

'The blood...' he said, pointing at her arm.

'Oh...' Gilda said, rubbing at the red mark near her elbow.

'It's nothing– it's not mine. I was birthing Mr Clarke's son.'

'I see. Then I will bother you no further.'

'Blue Sky,' Gilda said, standing from her spot on the grass and staring at him. She moved closer but he took a step back, at once realising his folly in returning here. He could not let himself get close to her. It was hard enough seeing her again after hours of being apart and thinking of nothing but the way her tender body had quivered in his heavy hands. If he caught even the slightest trace of her scent he would pull her into him and never want to let her go. Why torture himself when she was leaving? Just like his mother had and everyone else would, given enough time.

'Blue Sky,' she tried again. 'I'm so tired right now I could cry. Please, test me no longer. If something has aggrieved you then –'

'I am sorry if I don't like being toyed with,' he said, unable to look at her. Even as he uttered the words he knew he was being unreasonable. He had heard her just minutes ago defending his kind to Arabella. But he had seen the truth in her eyes when she denied their being together. She thought he was beneath her.

'How can you say that? In what way have I toyed with you?'

'Yesterday, you made me believe you truly desired me.'

'I did... I do...'

'It didn't seem so when Lawson accused you of trifling with me. I saw the look in your eyes. You are ashamed of me.'

Gilda stared hard at Blue Sky for a long moment before shaking her head and walking past him.

'Where are you going?'

'To my bed.'

'You won't deny it then – I am right in what I think?'

'No,' Gilda turned on him and for the first time since they met she raised her voice. Knowing he deserved her wrath only made it worse. 'You are not right. But I don't really need to tell you that. You know in your heart that I was putting on a show for Lawson and Clarke.'

'That is what I thought at first. But I saw –'

'I had to be convincing,' Gilda cut him off. 'Do you know what they would have done to you if they had any proof at all that we had tangled? Lawson would find a way of contriving it was against my will or would have rallied all the other townsmen to hunt you down as payback for stealing a white woman.

I was trying to protect you, but you are determined to always think the worst in me. You told me a Shawnee warrior is trained to be fearless. But you are full of fear. You won't let anybody close, and I do not have the patience for being pushed away when I have shown nothing but kindness. Goodbye, Blue Sky.'

As she said this, Blue Sky watched tears form in her eyes and hated himself for being the cause of her pain. Part of him wanted to shout back at her for daring to suggest he was afraid but much as it galled him to concede it, she was right. He would not usually get so confused around a woman. He would lie with them, show them their due respect and then withdraw. But with Gilda he found he was at war with himself. Perhaps because he had not seen such sweetness in a white person in a very long time, and that made him weak for her in a way that struck terror into his heart. What scared him more than anything however, was the sight of her walking away. He dodged around her, standing in her path. She changed direction and tried to walk around him but again he stopped her.

'What do you want?' she said, with a sigh.

Slowly, he reached out and brushed a strand of hair from her face. A single tear slipped down her cheek as he did so. He swiped it away and gathered her up in his arms.

'I am sorry,' he said, kissing her head. 'Forgive me.' He could not believe he was saying those words to a white woman but he was and he meant them, completely. 'I am punishing you for things you did not do. I am being unfair. But, so much happened before you came into my life.'

'I know,' Gilda said, tracing a fingertip along his jaw. Her touch was so gentle. How could he hate such a kindly creature? 'Great Hawk told me about what happened to your mother and how you haven't let anyone close to you since.'

Blue Sky was surprised to feel moisture on his cheek and then realised it was his own tears. More threatened but he swallowed them back while Little Sun kissed his cheeks where the others had fallen.

'They wanted to use me as a slave, your people,' he said, once he had recovered himself. 'But my mother wouldn't permit them to take me away. So they stoned her to death. There was no trial for her killers.'

'My precious man,' Gilda said, staring up at him. Her eyes filled with grief on his behalf. 'I wish I could do something to take that pain away.'

'When I'm with you...' Blue Sky stopped himself. Was he really going to admit this? That when he was with her the pain he had felt for as long as he could remember felt farther away? No. He could accept it privately but he wasn't ready to speak it. He looked around the empty streets. The sun was close to rising. People would soon be awake and they couldn't be seen together like this. And yet, he was not ready to part. Some small voice inside asked him if he would ever be ready to part with her. 'Let me take you away somewhere,' he said at last. 'Just far enough that we can be together for a while.'

'I want to,' Gilda said, 'But after the night I've had I fear I may do nothing more than fall asleep in your arms.'

Blue Sky smiled and whispered into Gilda's ear. 'Then I will watch over you and braid your hair while you sleep.'

'Oh, goodness. Be careful,' Gilda said with a small smile. 'If you do that I might very well fall in love with you. Then you'll be sorry.'

Fall in love? Why didn't those words fill him with the usual foreboding? And how was this woman so open and free with her feelings? At Little Sun's words, Blue Sky ached to say something bold in return. Something that would let her know he wouldn't mind her falling in love with him. But he couldn't get the sounds past his teeth. Despite her humorous comment, she had already made it clear that her future lay where he was not. So instead of saying anything, he reached out his hand. She put her hand in his and he interlocked their fingers as they walked towards his horse.

He helped her onto the animal first and then climbed up behind her, gripping her curvaceous body as he commanded his ride into a trot. He could sense from the way she leaned against him that his Little Sun was tired and he would, as promised, watch over her while she slept. Once she awoke however, he would find ways to make his earlier foolishness a distant memory. He couldn't help but notice how good she felt propped against his body nor could he resist passing his hand around her waist, squeezing her closer. As he did so he began to wonder if he should accept her leaving for New Orleans. Perhaps if he treated her as well as she deserved, she would stay here with him. At least long enough for them to discover what they had. Blue Sky's lips twitched into a smile as he began imagining all the tricks he might use to try to change her mind about her journey south.

# CHAPTER FIFTEEN

ilda awoke a few hours later, grinning as she at once sensed the comforting strength of Blue Sky's arms around her. Drowsily, she stared up at him. He lay propped against a large rock in a glade some ride from the town. She lounged between his legs. Her head rested on his chest. They were sheltered by a ring of leafy water oaks which meant she had him all to herself. It felt so comfortable and secure to lie like this. In truth she never thought she could feel this way whilst lying in a man's arms. She kissed the soft skin around his bared nipple then looked up at him again. His blue eyes twinkled for the first time since they had met. She would have paid good money to know what he was thinking about right then.

'Are you hungry?' Blue Sky whispered.

'That's pretty much a given for me at any time of day.'

Kissing her forehead, Blue Sky leaned forward and manoeuvred his way out from behind her. Gilda at once regretted admitting she was hungry. Had she known that rectifying the problem would mean being released from his arms she would have stuck it out and stayed quiet. She only had limited time to be with Blue Sky, she did not want to fritter it away with eating arrangements.

Mercifully, he did not stray far. Only a few paces to his satchel, from which he pulled a leather pouch.

'Hold out your hand,' he instructed, then poured a generous heap of nuts and berries into her palm.

'Perfect,' Gilda said, tossing the delicious morsels into her mouth one-by-one. Blue Sky crouched next to her, watching until she had finished and then sat beside her, taking some lengths of her hair into his hands.

'Oh, you were serious about the braiding,' Gilda said, with a chuckle. 'I thought you were just trying to charm me.'

'Both might be true,' Blue Sky said, making Gilda laugh harder.

'Can I ask, why were you in Williamsburg this morning?' Gilda said. 'I mean, were you there to see me?'

'I planned to deliver a gift to your porch last night but when I arrived, I saw Clarke rousing the household. As you were awake, and I thought I may never see you again, I waited until the disturbance was over with the intention of giving you the gift in person.'

Gilda grabbed Blue Sky's hand and turned to him. 'I would not have left without saying goodbye.'

'I may have made that difficult for you,' he said, knotting her braid at the end. 'Ridden off for a few days when you were due to leave.'

'In which case I would have written you a letter telling you that your stubbornness had cost you the most passionate goodbye kiss you would ever have received, and possibly a lot more.'

Blue Sky, cupped Gilda's face in his hands. He opened his mouth to speak but then, just as he had back in town closed his mouth again.

'Whatever you cannot bring yourself to say, it may be best if you say it. I won't be here forever.'

'Perhaps you don't want to hear it.'

'If it is something that you think or feel, then I want to hear it,' she said. It was painful to watch him, struggling with the weight of words he had never found a way to express.

'Yesterday when I went for Lawson. When you intervened. When I nearly...' He trailed off and looked at her. 'I would never hurt you on purpose.'

'I know that,' Gilda said, unable to stand even the small physical distance between them any longer. She was up on her knees in an instant and then straddled his lap so she could press herself close to him and hold his face in her hands. 'It was an accident.'

'But I nearly killed you.'

'But you didn't. I believe in the sharp instincts of my Shawnee warrior.'

He wrapped his arms around her and squeezed her close. He had come so very close to ending her life yesterday. She had seen the wild fury in his eyes as he had stormed towards her and stopped the knife only at the last moment. It had startled her, she couldn't deny that. But had the worst happened, it would have been a terrible accident not the deliberate cruelty she was used to.

'Defence is a different matter,' he said. 'But I swear to you I will never again raise my knife so swiftly in attack.'

Gilda nodded. 'I believe you.'

'So, you forgive me?'

'It was already forgiven. It's hard to think of holding any grudge against you for long.'

'How can you... be like that? Say what you feel so honestly?'

Gilda smiled to bide time. How did she answer that question without telling him everything? 'My life was difficult back in England,' she said. 'I promised myself when I came to America that I would seize every day. Take every chance. Live and speak freely, and without regret. Of course, I had no idea I would meet you and my philosophy would so soon be put to the test.'

There, that was a truthful explanation. Granted, she had omitted that her hedonistic values were part fuelled by the fact that she could never be sure when her past might catch-up with her and make the day she was living now her last. But it was as honest she could be without placing him in unnecessary danger.

'That is a fine way to live,' Blue Sky said. 'In that spirit there is something I would like to say to you, Little Sun.'

She did her best not to visibly melt when he used that name for her, but it was a challenge.

'I'm listening.'

'I – I can't explain why but... I want you.'

'I think I've made it more than clear that I want you too.'

'No, I mean, I want to know what it feels like to... be inside you.'

Gilda's eyelashes fluttered at that thought.

'But I cannot ask that. There is medicine but it does not always work and if I give you a baby, you may not know about it until you are far from here.'

'I don't think you will give me a baby,' said Gilda, her stomach tightening all of a sudden at the thought of what she was about to say. Even under different circumstances, or in some far off future there was no hope for her and Blue Sky. What man would want a woman who could not give him a child?

'What do you mean by this?' he asked, frowning.

Gilda took in a deep breath. Considering again how much she should tell Blue Sky. 'I gave myself to one man back in England and another took what he wanted from me against my will, more than once. And as you can see I remain childless.'

'Who is this man? Who took you against your will?' Blue Sky's voice had a sudden fierceness that made it clear if he ever got his hands on *him*, he was unlikely to live to tell of it. Another reason to be sparing with the details. Despite his aloof façade it was obvious Blue Sky was protective by nature and would likely go to battle for her honour. She didn't need that on her conscience, not on top of everything else.

'He is far from here and not worth another thought,' she said.

If only she could follow her own advice.

She had thought of him many times since she had set sail from London. His mocking glare often surfaced in her mind when she least expected and sometimes she wondered if she would ever forget the things he did to her.

'Are you telling me you cannot have a child?' said Blue Sky.

'That's what I believe.'

'Which means we could be together?'

'We could,' Gilda said, 'But there are other concerns besides babies.'

'What are they?'

'Disease,' Gilda answered frankly. It would be a different matter if I were staying and we were to develop a relationship but with a union so fleeting we would be foolish to risk passing on ailments to one another. Especially as I come from a place filled with maladies you have no tolerance to. I might be gone by the time symptoms show, which means I would not be able to treat you.'

'I should be willing to take the risk,' Blue Sky said, running his hands through her hair.

Gilda laughed. 'I do not doubt it. You have not seen the things a doctor's daughter has seen.'

'So, we cannot be together?'

'In truth, there is a solution. My father prescribed a silk sheath for his gentleman patients who visited whores behind their wife's back.'

'Such nobles you have in England,' Blue Sky said dryly.

'Yes, again being a physician you become accustomed to the less pleasant side of people's lives.'

'These sheaths… you wear them…' Blue Sky nodded towards his groin.

'Yes. I have some in my medical bag.' Gilda cursed herself for handing her bag to Arabella. It was too cumbersome to keep on her person but if she had managed that small burden, Blue Sky could have been inside her right then.

'Do you want to go that far with me, my Little Sun? I am not like that other man you knew. It is only pleasurable to me if it is pleasurable to you.'

'How could I not want you?' Gilda whispered, before running her fingers through his hair. 'We could make plans for tonight. Once second sleep has begun. I could creep out of the room without Arabella knowing a thing.'

'And then I could bring you here… and be with you?'

Gilda nodded. Her breath deepening at the thought.

'Then it is agreed. But in the meantime,' Blue Sky said, with a rakish smile. 'I should like to find other ways to pleasure you.'

# CHAPTER SIXTEEN

lue Sky aligned his arm along Gilda's spine and gripped the base of her neck before slowly easing her onto her back. She lay there, in the long grasses, her skin pinkening and her eyes widening as he untied his breechcloth and threw it aside. Once disrobed he lay on top of her again, being careful to put just enough of his weight on her for it to be pleasurable. He ran his fingertips along the bridge of her nose and over her lips, thinking about all she had confessed to him. A man had taken her against her will, more than once. And yet she offered herself to him in the most placid and trusting manner. He would not let her regret that choice. He would bed her tonight and make her forget that man ever callously defiled her. When he was finished, she would know in her heart she had made the right choice to lie with him. But to do that, to show her he was different to the men she had known before, he needed to know exactly what she wanted.

Slowly, he slipped his hands up her petticoats, brushing the back of his hands against the softness of her skin before parting her thighs. A short gasp escaped Little Sun's full lips as he pushed his stiffness against her.

'Oh my Little Sun,' he hissed. 'You are already so... so...'

'I know,' she part-gasped. 'It's what you do to me. It's what happens when I think of you inside of me.'

At her words, Blue Sky began to gently thrust his hips against hers. She arched her body to meet him and the pair let out an almost agonized moan.

'What do you want me to do with you tonight?' Blue Sky said, keeping his thrusts gentle but steady. The feel of her nook, so warm and wet, sliding down the length of his shaft was driving him wild. If this is how he felt now, how was he going to handle it when he was pounding his way inside her with deep, long strokes? Thankfully, Little Sun spoke and distracted him from that line of thought which would likely result in a very swift end to his enjoyment of her.

'I want you to undress me, slowly, so you can see every inch of me.'

That idea alone caused Blue Sky's movements to quicken. 'I should not just want to look at you. No part of you will go unkissed.'

'No part?' Gilda said, her cheeks turning an even deeper shade of pink than before.

'Not your shoulder, nor your elbow, nor the sweet spot between your parted buttocks.'

Little Sun's eyes widened further at his description but as her rippling against his body became harder and more deliberate he was sure he had not over-stepped.

'The thought of your tongue in those places... there aren't words. At least, none that a lady can utter,' she said, and then between increasingly desperate panting added, 'I would want to explore you with my mouth too, every inch of you.'

Blue Sky growled as he remembered how tightly her little mouth had fit around his rod. How far she had let him bury his way inside her. He imagined her whole body would be just as snug a sheath.

'How should I enter you, tonight?' he asked, unable to pretend that he could think about anything else. Her nectar was pooling around his pole now and the sensation was driving him wild.

'Slowly, at first,' she said. 'So I can savour the feeling of you pushing your way inside me, and the sight of that breathtaking body. I want you to kiss me, as you enter.'

'That was a given,' he said, knowing he would never miss an opportunity to cover her mouth with his own.

'I want to feel our bodies as close as they possibly can be,' she said, 'and then, once we have connected, I don't want you to hold back.'

'Say more.'

'I want you to take me…ride me… as hard and as fast and as long as you can.'

Blue Sky was aware his jaw was hanging open at her request but he could not muster the strength to close it. The image of her body, her breasts, her flesh shaking to his most urgent rhythm brought him to the edge and it seemed she was not far behind.

'Oh, my precious man, you like that idea,' she said her body beginning to quake as he rubbed his manhood against her with increased speed. 'Oh it's too much. I want you too much. I'm going to… to…' Little Sun screamed and dug her fingernails hard into his back as she reached the height of her pleasure. Unable to hold on any longer amid the sound and the scent of her arousal, Blue Sky followed her lustful cue and spilled his seed over her stomach, moaning as he felt it soak into her once-pristine cotton shift. Spent, he fell on top of her, gasping and still groaning from his remembered ecstasy.

'Oh goodness,' Little Sun said, after he delivered a soft, slow kiss. 'I've got a terrible feeling I am in genuine trouble with you.'

Blue Sky smiled down at her and let out a long, deep chuckle. 'My Little Sun, I am glad I am the one to teach you that some trouble is worth getting into.'

# CHAPTER SEVENTEEN

'id Blue Sky give you that?' Arabella asked. Her tone was a little more cautious than usual after their argument that morning, and had been for the remainder of the day.

Gilda stared at her maid in the cold moonlight, unsure how to answer. It was clear to anyone that the poppet resting on her knee, a rudimentary figure cut from raw hide and stuffed with buffalo hair, had been crafted by native hands. With second sleep just an hour away, it was unlikely that Arabella would have chance to pass on anything Gilda told her. If she even hinted to Widow Westerby that Gilda had affections for Blue Sky however, that might be enough to draw unwanted attention. She did not want anything to get in the way of the tryst she had agreed with her native lover that evening.

'It is a gift sent from Great Hawk for my healing of him,' Gilda said, with a small smile. That, Blue Sky had admitted, was the story he was going to tell her about the doll when he still valued his pride over his honesty with her. In truth, it was a gift from him alone. He wanted the doll to comfort her after the passing of her father during times he was not present to do so. When she learned that this doll had brought him great relief when his mother was taken from him, she tried to refuse the gift. Only when he insisted that refusing would offend him did she acquiesce and tuck the precious little figure in her pocket. For much of the day, when nobody was looking, she had run her fingertips over the soft hide. Imagining Blue Sky as a young boy, clutching the doll close, her heart fluttering at the thought that he had bestowed something on her that was so much a part of him.

After she had awoken from first sleep, she had thought she would be safe to admire Blue Sky's offering while sitting out on the porch step. With Arabella awake and in proximity, she should have known better.

Her maid sat beside her on the stoop.

'I do 'ate it when I displease you, Miss,' she said.

'I know, you did not do so on purpose.'

'I 'eard what Mr Lawson said about the natives and got carried away. But I've been thinking about it all day and if you say they are not to be feared, well, that's good enough for me.'

'Spend long enough in their company and you won't have to take my word for it,' Gilda said.

A silence fell over the two women.

'Mistress,'

'Mmm?'

'You're in love with him, aren't you? Blue Sky.' Arabella's voice was very quiet as she asked this. There was still a note of restraint. Gilda suspected her maid was surprised at how she had flared up at what were to her mind widely accepted assumptions about the natives, and that is what had given her affections away. She looked into Arabella's green sparkling eyes. There was no malice or mockery in them, only kindness. She shook her head.

'Don't be silly, Bella. A person cannot love another that quickly.'

'Maybe not,' Arabella said, her eyes narrowing. 'But you're going that way. I can tell.'

'I never knew you were such an expert,' Gilda said, doing what she could to keep the tone light in the hope she could steer Arabella away from this particular topic.

'Oh, I know more than you know I know,' Arabella said with a proud nod.

Gilda couldn't help but chuckle. 'Well, that's fixed then. When we get to our final destination I shall have you assess all my suitors.'

Arabella laughed but then sobered. 'I'm sorry I asserted myself with Blue Sky. I didn't know then, that you felt for him.'

Gilda put an arm around her maid's shoulders. She had not had cause to touch her in this manner before but the young girl did not resist her friendliness. 'Of course you didn't. I've done such a good job of keeping my affections for Blue Sky hidden.'

Arabella laughed and rubbed Gilda's arm.

A deep voice suddenly startled them. 'Briar Chatterton?' it said.

At once, Gilda was on her feet and she spun towards the person who had spoken. Blue Sky was standing just at the end of the porch. By the lantern she could make out the hardened lines of his face.

Without a word, he turned on his heel and strode away.

There was only one way Blue Sky could have heard that name.

*He* was here.

Gilda's eyes widened and her whole body began to tremble. 'Bella, go inside the house,' she said in a low voice.

'But –'

'Now!' Gilda shouted. 'Bolt the door. Do not to open it to anyone but me.'

# CHAPTER EIGHTEEN

ehind him, Blue Sky could hear Gilda, or Briar or whatever her name was instructing Arabella to go inside the house. There was some back and forth but ultimately the maid did as instructed and the next thing he heard was the scuffing of her skirt against the dusty ground as she ran after him.

'Blue Sky, please don't walk away. Not now.'

Despite the shock he had received, the pleading note in her voice was enough to slow him.

'Please, where did you hear that name?' she asked, stepping around him so they were standing face to face.

For the first time in as long as he could remember Blue Sky felt the urge to bellow. Most people were inside at this time of night but he could not take the risk that someone was sitting out on their porch between sleeps, just as she had been. 'I cannot stay and talk with you when you were going to lie with me and not even tell me your real name. I thought you trusted me.'

Gilda shook her head. 'My darling man it was not a matter of trust. I was worried that if I told you my real name and he came asking after me you might give yourself away without even realising it… and he's dangerous and… he's here, isn't he? That's how you know. He's here.'

At those words all colour drained from her face and it was only then that he noticed her whole body was shaking. He wanted to ignore her obvious fear but she was too far under his skin now. Even if she had lied to him, she was still a woman scared and alone with an unrelenting thug tailing her across continents.

Unable to stop himself, Blue Sky encircled her in his arms. She looked up at him, her eyes wide and filled with tears. 'Briar, Gilda, it doesn't matter what other names I've gone by. I am y*our* Little Sun. Please… please believe me.'

'I do,' he said, though in truth he was still unsure what to believe. The only thing he knew for certain just then was that she needed comfort and when she looked so lost he couldn't bear to deny her.

He smoothed his hands over her hair. 'I was in the tavern with Fast River when he walked in. He asked if the owner knew a Briar Chatterton. He went on to describe you down to every detail. When the owner made it clear he had not heard of nor seen a Briar Chatterton this man began to circulate, questioning others. I left before he could ask anything of me. Fast River is still there, keeping watch on him.'

A panicked look crossed her face and Blue Sky briefly held up a hand to reassure her.

'Fast River will not reveal any details to the man. But Little Sun, who is he?'

She swallowed hard and took a deep breath before answering. 'His name is Marcus Gaunt. He works for a Bank back in England… He…' she paused, blinking back tears. 'He is the man I told you of, who took more from me than I wanted.'

Blue Sky's fists at once tightened to knots. In his heart he had known that was the case and as such had nearly ended the man's life where he stood in the tavern. The only thing that stopped him had been the knowledge that he was outnumbered by white men and if he died, the bastard might get to his Little Sun, and there would be nothing he could do to stop him.

'Why is he here?' said Blue Sky.

'I was… supposed to marry him,' Little Sun said. 'It's why I left. It's why I… did a lot of things. Please understand, in the beginning he was a gentleman. My father was getting worried that I wouldn't find a match. So I agreed to marry him. But then, Gaunt changed. He became dangerously possessive and wanted to know my whereabouts every minute of the day. It's hard to explain how it all happened. I am a spirited woman.'

'I have seen that for myself.'

'Then you understand I am not some mouse a man can easily intimidate. But it happened slowly. He was sly. It got to the point that he would only allow me to leave my house in his company. I tried to break the engagement and he told me if I did he would hurt my family. I couldn't bear the idea of anyone I loved paying the price for my short-sightedness so... I agreed to stay. He then told me if I ever lied to him about where I was or what I was doing, he'd find me and kill me. One night he invited me to his house and took my virginity. He said he was just taking what was his a little bit early. He took from me several nights after that.'

With every sentence Little Sun uttered Blue Sky's muscles clenched tighter. He understood how Little Sun, and all of her peers, might have been fooled by Gaunt. He had entered the tavern in a tan jacket and breeches looking every bit the English gentleman with his blonde hair tied back with a black ribbon. His manner to the guests at the tavern had been more than cordial. Nobody would suspect he was capable of the behaviour Little Sun described.

'How did you get away?'

'One day he told me he had taken me before the wedding night because he didn't want to delay working on an heir.'

'He didn't know you were unable to give him that.'

'Neither did I, at the time,' she said. 'I was petrified that I would conceive a child by that… that… monster. I tried to escape several times. Told my father I was going to visit friends. But every time Gaunt caught me and, scared for my life, I had no choice but to beg his forgiveness.'

'Oh, my Little Sun,' Blue Sky said, wishing he had been there back in England to rescue her from the brute. 'I take it one of your escape attempts did work?'

'I wasn't brave enough for that at first,' she admitted. 'At first I tried to think of easier solutions. I assumed that if he believed I'd given him an heir he might ease off with his behaviour. So… I asked an old friend of mine to lie with me.'

'Little Sun… you didn't?'

'I couldn't stand to bear Gaunt's child. I was desperate. But when I bled the next month as usual I started to suspect I couldn't have a child which would surely mean a life of torture with a man like Gaunt.'

'So what did you do?'

'One day he had the bad sense to blacken my eye. Andrew noticed and told my father. I begged them not to confront Gaunt. I had seen what he was capable of.'

'Could they not go to your courts?'

Little Sun looked at Blue Sky as though he was crazed but then her expression softened. 'The law in England does not protect women against their fiancés and husbands, especially not over a black eye. Even if I could convince a magistrate that Gaunt had wronged me, he would be fined twelve pence and I would be sent back home with him.'

Blue Sky now understood the look she had given him. Her society had watched on as this man had abused her before she was even wed and offered her no way out. 'So what did you do?'

'It got to the point where I realised the only way to get away from him was to die. So I died.'

'I don't understand.'

'I left him a note saying that I intended to drown myself in the river. My father organised my passage to America and my brother agreed to conduct a funeral after my disappearance to make it seem final. I did not want to leave my family. I did not want to come to the New World, especially after reading my grandfather's letters, but my brother and father convinced me it was my best chance of a new life. They feared that if Gaunt learnt I couldn't bear an heir he would find a way to get rid of me. So,' Little Sun said, taking a deep breath, 'that is why, you see, I am not Briar Chatterton. She is long dead.'

Blue Sky was quiet for a moment digesting all she had told him.

'Do not worry,' Little Sun continued, filling the silence. 'I do not expect you to understand or forgive the many deceits I carried out to escape him. But I hope you know that I only went to such lengths because I was in despair.' Little Sun scraped her fingers through her blonde hair. 'There is no time to lose. I will spend the next few hours packing. At first light I will organise passage for myself and Arabella to New Orleans. You will not have to see me again.'

'Is that what you want? To leave?'

'It was the plan. But no, I don't wish to leave. I would rather stay here and find out what happens between you and me.'

Blue Sky nodded. 'Then I will kill him, and you will stay.'

'You can't do that,' Little Sun said in a quiet voice.

'Why not?'

'Because it's wrong.'

'What about all he has done to you? Is that not wrong?'

'Yes, but that doesn't make killing him right.'

'Yes, it does.'

'No... I wish it did. You have no idea how much I wish that. If I could live with myself afterwards, you can be sure I'd be first in line to kill him after all he has done to me. But I can't.'

'I can.'

'I won't let you risk a lynching, or let you get blood on your hands on my account. Don't you see? If you kill him you become more like him. Willing to use any means to get what you want. I am a doctor. I don't end life and I cannot sanction the ending of another life, even his.'

Blue Sky did not want to acknowledge her argument but he admitted privately that it made sense. His Little Sun wanted nothing to do with Gaunt and if he killed the man for his crimes, she would want nothing to do with him either.

'Must you leave so soon?'

Little Sun nodded.

'So we can't… we can't be together.'

Little Sun shook her head and leaned to kiss him. He did not resist but pushed her around to the side of the yellow house and pinned her hard up against the end wall. He lifted her off the ground, just by an inch or two, so their bodies were better aligned. So she could feel his stiffness rubbing against her stomach. She whimpered and drove her hips into his. This was almost enough for him to forget everything he had just said and end Gaunt anyway. But then he focused on the soft lips of the lady in his arms. The scent of roses that filled his lungs. The softness of her rounded curves filling his big hands. He could not break a promise to a woman like this.

'I'm sorry,' she said when their lips at last parted. 'It may seem like a rash thing to say but I may never see you again and I want you to know. I've never been in love before but I really do think I could have fallen in love with you.'

Blue Sky responded with another deep kiss, wishing he could verbalise his need for her to stay. As he gripped her slender neck and pulled at her long, blonde hair however he decided this would not be goodbye. She did not know it yet but she would be kissing him for many days to come. The moment she was indoors, he would make his way straight back to that tavern to keep watch on Gaunt. If he was the terror Little Sun believed him to be, and he had no doubt she was right, then the man would slip up soon enough and if he could gather evidence of Gaunt's wrong doings Mr Clarke might actually step up and do his duty. As she reached a hand down to his hardened pole straining against his breech-cloth, he vowed that he and his Little Sun would be together. Just as he had fought for his people, he would fight for her, if that is what it took, until his dying breath.

# CHAPTER NINETEEN

At the yellow house, beyond a small sitting room, there was a modest kitchen with a rickety old table and three rickety chairs to match. This is where Gilda could be found early the next morning. Re-examining the maps her father had bestowed upon her before she left for America, which she planned to use to travel more than one thousand miles to New Orleans. Pressing her fingertips against the pencilled markings, she realised that these maps were the last gift her father would ever give her. Between that thought, the arrival of Gaunt and her separation from Blue Sky happening sooner than expected it was becoming difficult to blink back the tears that had threatened for the last six hours.

There had been no knock at the door yet and so long as Gaunt didn't talk to anyone who might recognise her description anytime soon, they should be able to slink out of Williamsburg without him knowing a thing about it. For once, the man's heavy drinking was going to work in her favour. Unless he was in at the bank, he never could rouse himself before midday after an evening of steady inebriation. If he had been at the tavern all night, she had some time on her side before he awoke from his stupor. At least, that's what Gilda had been counting on until Arabella came in from the porch.

'Mistress, there was a letter sitting outside for you,' she said. Gilda noticed Arabella's hand shaking as she passed over the cream envelope. Her once-cheery maid had been rattled by the truths Gilda had divulged about the man who was after her. She wished she could do something to calm the poor girl's fears but she could not be sure what Gaunt was capable of. She only knew, she couldn't go back to him. No matter what.

Gilda accepted the envelope but, when she marked the handwriting, dropped it onto the table with dismay as though it were a copperhead. It belonged to Gaunt. He had found her.

'Did you bolt the door?' Gilda asked urgently.

'Yes Miss, all locked up.'

Gilda tried to steady her breathing. Perhaps the contents of this envelope were not as bad as she feared. Perhaps someone in the town had talked sense in to him and the letter was merely an apologetic goodbye. These were the stories she told herself as she lifted the flap on the envelope and pulled out the letter enclosed.

*Dear Gilda – I hear that is the name you go by these days.*

*I hope you are not too attached to that name because you will soon be exchanging it for the much more upstanding title of Mrs M. Gaunt. How overjoyed our friends in Lincoln will be when they discover you were not dead after all but kidnapped to the New World by* a ruthless team of bandits. And how they will all revere me for ensuring your safe return.

Mr Lawson, who recognised not your name but my description of you, has apprised me of your exploits in the short time you have been in Williamsburg. It sounds as though you have been busy. Indeed, it seems as though you have gone to all possible lengths to humiliate your future husband.

Naturally, I will not stand for this wickedness. I have your Indian lover. He is alive, for now. If you wish for him to see another sunrise you will come to me tonight at 9 o clock to the point I have marked on the map drawn below. I doubt anyone would care much about the kidnap of a savage but in case you do get it into your little birdbrain to report it, you should know I have people watching Mr Clarke who, I am informed, is the magistrate around here. I also have people watching the savage's village. If you inform anyone I will kill the impertinent half-breed and then come after you. Either way, you, my little hussy, will pay a heavy price for the disgrace you have caused me.

*I expect to see you soon,*

*M. Gaunt.*

Gilda had never been so grateful to be seated for if she had been standing she would surely have fallen to the floor in pure shock. As it was she let the letter flutter to the table and put her head in her hands.

'He's got Blue Sky,' she said her voice quiet, her thoughts turning to that passionate man whom she had held in her arms but hours ago.

She frowned then. How had Gaunt managed to capture Blue Sky? Even with Mr Lawson's help, Gilda couldn't imagine them overpowering her warrior. She had felt the power of his muscles for herself. His instincts were razor sharp on any ordinary day and after all she had told him about Gaunt he would surely be on his guard.

Perhaps Gaunt was just bluffing. Perhaps he didn't have Blue Sky at all and his claims were merely bait. Without being able to ride out to the Indian village, she couldn't know for sure.

Arabella picked up the note, small gasps escaping her at regular intervals as she read it to herself. 'What are we going to do?'

'We are not going to change our plan,' Gilda said after a moment. 'In a few hours, Mr Brownlow will have arranged passage to Bath for us. By the time nine o clock comes we will be well on our way to New Orleans and it will be too late for Gaunt to pick up our trail.'

'What about Blue Sky? Do you think 'e'll kill him?'

'I think it's a bluff,' said Gilda. Perhaps if she said those words loud enough they would feel real. 'And even if it is not, I don't believe Blue Sky would want us to go out there and put ourselves in danger when the odds are he will find some means of escape.'

She told herself again that Blue Sky was the strongest man she had ever known and had a reputation as a person not to be crossed. Even if they had managed to capture him, Gaunt and Lawson wouldn't keep him for long.

An emptiness mushroomed within and she almost changed her mind about leaving, but she couldn't return to Gaunt. She couldn't be defiled that way; controlled that way for the rest of her life. She had spent all of her days helping others. For once, she had to do what was best for herself.

'Not a word to anyone about that letter, do you hear me?'

'Yes, Miss,' Arabella said.

'Go and check on Mr Brownlow,' Gilda added, ignoring the look of disbelief on Arabella's face. 'See if he can arrange for passage to Bath any earlier than planned.'

# CHAPTER TWENTY

The sun was high when Blue Sky's eyes finally prised open. Frowning, he tried to get a sense of his surroundings. He recognised this spot in the woods. He had spent some time hunting in this small clearing just a few miles south of the town. The relief of recognising his location was soon replaced by panic as he tried to move and realised his hands were tied behind his back. Looking down he saw that his feet, like his hands, were secured to a metal stake – as tall as he was – dug deep into the ground. How had he got here? Why couldn't he remember? He began to struggle with the ropes that bound his wrists.

'I wouldn't bother tryin' that half-breed,' Lawson drawled, appearing from the woods. He was closely followed by the man who had taken Little Sun's dignity. The sight of him only made Blue Sky struggle harder.

'You tire yourself out if you wish, savage,' said Gaunt. 'If you're exhausted as well as restrained it will be all the easier to kill you when the time comes.'

'Huh. I could kill him with or without restraints, exhausted or fresh from a restful sleep,' said Lawson.

'Then untie me, so you can prove it,' Blue Sky growled.

Gaunt let out a long, cold cackle that was enough for him to know he would not be untied.

Again, Blue Sky pulled against the ropes, but they were too tight. This told him, at least, that they feared him. That they understood if he managed to escape that would be the end of them, and on that point they were not mistaken. He had been willing to play fair on Little Sun's behalf but they were not playing by the same rules. So now, if he got his chance, he would gladly kill them. Perhaps he could find a way to use their fear against them? Maybe even bait them into arguing and killing each other – or at least roughing each other up enough to give him the physical advantage.

'I trust you didn't get your hopes up too far about Briar's affections for you,' Gaunt said. He pulled a small flask from his coat pocket and took a quick swig.

That's right, Blue Sky thought. Get rotten drunk. It will be easier to beat you down.

'You surely know she doesn't belong with a scarred little ruffian like you,' Gaunt continued. 'I know why she picked you out. As a physician, she's never been able to resist trying to fix lame dogs. But her attraction to you, I'm afraid, goes no deeper than pity.'

Blue Sky knew better than to respond. Even though Gaunt's words struck the most sensitive nerve he had when it came to his Little Sun – the knowledge that when it came down to it he could not offer a life good enough for her – he had to conserve his energy and think. Did anyone know he was here? Would anyone at the village notice he was missing? Fast River had been drinking with him at the tavern. He remembered that much. He had been watching Gaunt, waiting for him to do something he might go to Mr Clarke about. But then Fast River had decided return home to his wife. Fast River would not worry about Blue Sky's absence for some days. He was known for galloping off on his own as it suited him. He could not hope for rescue from his people.

So, Fast River had left him alone in the tavern. Blue Sky had stayed for a few more drinks. Nowhere near his limits. But that was the last thing he remembered. Drinking alone in the tavern. The aching of his ribs and face told him that however he had been transported here the method had been far from gentle.

'What's the matter, savage?' said Lawson. 'You're not full of your usual wise-cracks.'

'If I know the beady, savage mind I would say he's plotting his escape,' said Gaunt. 'Let me save you some time. Those ropes are as tight as they can be. We made sure of it. Briar – or Gilda as you know her – will come here this evening believing that we'll let you go in exchange for her coming back to England with me.'

'She won't do that,' Blue Sky said, trying to ignore the stabbing pain through his heart as he said the words he believed to be true. 'She won't give her life for mine. She doesn't care for me enough for that.'

Gaunt shrugged. 'I'd rather do it the easy way but if she makes me I'll go after her and drag her back to England myself. I'm afraid tonight is the last time you'll see the stars, so I would look long at them if I were you. We'll tell Briar that we're going to cut you loose but you will die tonight, one way or the other. Nobody touches my woman the way you have and lives to talk about it.'

'She's too intelligent to believe your lies,' said Blue Sky.

'Maybe, but it's amazing what a person will believe if they are desperate enough,' said Gaunt. 'Mr Lawson, why don't you make sure when my beloved arrives that she's not under any illusions that this half-breed is in a condition to save her.'

'With pleasure,' Lawson said, puffing up his chest as he approached Blue Sky. As he took the first sickening blow to his already bruised ribs, as knuckle connected with bone, Blue Sky prayed to the Great Spirit that Little Sun did not come for him. Gaunt was being truthful about one thing: his binds were too tight to work himself free. If she did come to his aid on a fool's mission, it would surely be the end of them both.

# CHAPTER TWENTY-ONE

Later in the afternoon than Gilda would have liked, the coach finally pulled up outside the yellow house on Queen Street. The driver was loading their bags onto the vehicle when Gilda felt it in her pocket: the soft leather hide, stuffed with buffalo hair. A single tear slid down her cheek as she pulled out the small poppet and looked at it.

What was she doing? This doll had meant so much to him, and he had given it to her. Even knowing she was leaving. Even knowing she kept her secrets. He had given it to her as a comfort in difficult times and… now she was abandoning him? And worse, she was leaving Great Hawk's son to die, knowing, after the loss of his wife at the hands of her people, how alone the old man would be.

The thought of seeing Gaunt again, and being trapped in the life he would force her to lead, almost split her in two. But she could fool herself no longer. Deep down she knew it: Marcus had Blue Sky and if she didn't go to him, Blue Sky would die.

All breath left Gilda's lungs. She bent almost double with a strange, unquantifiable pain and let out a tortured shriek. 'I can't! I can't!'

'What is it Miss?' Arabella said in alarm.

'I can't... leave him.' The words shuddered out of her before she righted herself and bustled past a shocked-looking Widow Westerby. The old woman and Arabella followed her inside, rushing into the kitchen.

'What is it child? You've been agitated all morning. I thought it pure nerves about the long trip but there's more to it, isn't there?'

'I'm afraid there is, Goodie Westerby. And I'm afraid for your own health. Oh, I can't tell you it all now. If I go over it again I will lose what little nerve I have. Suffice to say that the person my father told you about, the one who wanted to hurt me: he is here in Williamsburg.'

'Oh Lord,' said Widow Westerby, lifting a hand to her head. 'Perhaps Mr Clarke can help?'

'We can't go to him,' Gilda said, remembering the words of Gaunt's letter. But then, a thought occurred to her. 'At least... not directly.'

With haste, Gilda opened her medical bag and pulled out her practitioner's notebook, her quill and some ink. She tore a page from the back of the book and began frantically dipping the quill, marking her words on the parchment. A moment later she rooted around for the letter Gaunt had sent, before opening it flat on the table, looking from that page to her own and scratching out words and lines at an almost hysterical pace.

'Do you have an idea, Miss?'

'No need to sound so surprised, Bella,' Gilda paused to say. 'I have had ideas before.'

Gilda continued writing for two more minutes and then grabbed the envelope that had contained Gaunt's letter and folded her paper inside.

'Bella, I need you to go to the market place. Here's a bag of shillings. Find someone to call on Mr Clarke's house and ask Elsie to meet you in the market square. When she comes, keep your demeanour light as though you are catching up on idle gossip. Laugh and chitter, do you hear me? And, when you are certain nobody is looking, slip her this envelope. Find a way to tell her it is imperative she hands it to Mr Clarke. Explain that my life, and Blue Sky's, depend on her discretion. Can you do this?'

'Of course Miss, whatever you say.'

'Goodie Westerby, I need you to keep the door bolted tight. Open it only to Bella before my departure. Here's some money for the coach driver's trouble. He will need to be sent away. And Mr Brownlow must be informed that I shall need one of his horses tonight ready to ride no later than eight o clock.

'What are you going to do?' Widow Westerby said, her voice wavering.

'I'm going to do what's right,' Gilda said, staring at the two women. 'I'm going to ride out and save my Blue Sky.'

# CHAPTER TWENTY-TWO

**B**lue Sky first knew that something of importance was happening when a rustling sounded in the foliage. Gaunt stood from the fallen log he'd been resting on, pulled a watch from his coat pocket and looked at it with an approving nod.

'I see your dalliance with the savage hasn't made you forget your English sensibilities. You are bang on time, my sweet.' Gaunt's tone was sly, mocking and each word had a slight slur to it. He hadn't drunk much since he sent Lawson away an hour ago, but before that he had more than his fill.

Blue Sky strained to turn his head just enough to confirm his worst fears. Little Sun emerged from the woodland in a scarlet dress and black cape, her golden hair braided down to her shoulders. Her eyes flashed with anger and were fixed on Gaunt. Blue Sky's blood froze in its veins. What the hell was she doing? Was she really alone? He craned his neck to look beyond her but saw nobody. He knew his Little Sun to be spirited, as she had described it, but facing Gaunt alone was nothing short of suicide.

Even after the beating Lawson had given him, had he not been restrained, he would have been able to fight long enough for her to get away. As it was, he couldn't even warn her that Lawson was somewhere around, for he had gagged Blue Sky just before he left. Gaunt and Lawson had been sure to turn their backs to him when discussing their plans but he could only think that Lawson was hiding out in the foliage, waiting to ambush her.

Yet again he struggled against his restraints and yet again they held firm. His movement caught Little Sun's eyes and she gasped as she hurried towards him.

'What have you done to him?' she shouted, taking in his comportment. He knew he was bruised and bloodied. He must look as worthless to her as Gaunt had intended. 'They cut off your hair?' Little Sun exclaimed further when she was close enough to see the full extent of their abuse. He had been close to tears when Lawson had taken a knife to the length of his locks. For his people, the growth of hair was akin to the growth of spirit. In three swift movements, Lawson had cut his short. The loss of his hair was almost as profound as the loss of his mother. He had vowed Lawson would pay but now Little Sun had appeared and all he could focus on was protecting her.

'We felt it important to teach the Indian more dignified ways,' Gaunt bit out.

'You will not lay another hand on this man,' Little Sun said, drawing a pistol from her skirt pocket.

A pistol? Where did Little Sun get a pistol? She must have loaded it already as she cocked the weapon and pointed it straight at Gaunt.

For his part, Gaunt let out a thick, deep cackle. 'You're not going to shoot me, girl. You don't even know how.'

'Andrew taught me. I can shoot you just fine.'

'Andrew,' Gaunt said through gritted teeth, 'will be going the same way as your father if he doesn't tread carefully.'

Little Sun frowned. 'What do you mean by that, Marcus?' When he didn't answer, she half-screamed again: 'What do you mean?'

Gaunt offered nothing more than a self-satisfied smirk. Just then Lawson lunged from a nearby bush. He grabbed Little Sun from behind and held his own pistol against her temple.

'Drop your weapon, girlie,' Lawson slimed. The mere sight of him pawing her was enough for Blue Sky to renew his pointless struggle against the binds.

Blue Sky watched in dread as her muscles slowly slackened and she admitted defeat. She dropped the pistol off to one side and Lawson dragged her towards Gaunt.

'Marcus, please,' she said to him. Blue Sky couldn't see her face but he could tell by the uneven tone of her voice that tears were close. 'Please tell me you didn't kill my father.'

'I didn't have much of a choice, did I? He wouldn't tell me where you were.'

'But I left you a note. Andrew held a funeral... how did you even know I was alive?'

A smug smile spread across Gaunt's lips. 'Think about it, Briar. I'm a banker. I know that if you follow the money sooner or later you find what you're looking for.'

'What?'

'Your bank manager Mr Gregory happens to be an acquaintance of mine. When I went to him as a concerned fiancé and explained that I suspected foul play regarding your disappearance he let me take a look at your account.'

Gilda's voice was quiet. 'You saw that I'd emptied my account the day before I disappeared.'

'That's right. If you were really going where you said you were going in that note, money wouldn't be any use to you. I knew I would find you but I also knew that when I got you back to Lincoln your father would be nothing but an interference.'

'So you killed him?' Little Sun said, struggling in vain against Lawson's iron grip. 'You... killed my father?'

'No, *you* killed your father. When you decided to humiliate me. When you ran from your wifely duties and, according to Mr Lawson's accounts, took up with this... this... animal.' Gaunt jabbed a finger in Blue Sky's direction.

'You are the animal,' Gilda said. Her voice had a low, deadly tone that Blue Sky had not heard before. Did she have a plan to overcome Gaunt, even without her pistol? Blue Sky prayed that she didn't. She had a fire in her but she was no match for the strength of two men.

'Don't worry,' Gaunt almost purred. 'I'm not heartless. I made it quick. Smothered him with a pillow while he slept. He would barely have known what was happening. All I had to do after that was wait for your brother to contact you about your father's death, which he did the next day, and find out where he had sent the letter. Not a difficult task when you've a few shillings to incentivise people.'

Little Sun was quiet for a good few moments. When she spoke again her voice was close to breaking.

'I *hate* you. You can't possibly believe I will voluntarily return to England with you after this admission?'

'Whether you come voluntarily is of little concern to me,' Gaunt said. 'I didn't suffer a seventy day voyage to go back to England empty-handed. Your father had some interesting substances in his medical case. I took the liberty of hanging on to his supply of opium. The same stuff I used to drug your lover's drink last night. It will work just as well on you.'

Blue Sky's muscles clenched. So Gaunt had drugged him, that's how they had overcome him and why he didn't remember what happened. But how? He hadn't accepted a drink from Gaunt? He must have made some arrangement with the barkeep to contaminate his drink. Was there any white man in this town with honour left in them?

Little Sun shook her head. 'Why can't you just... let me go?'

'Because, sweet, there have been whispers that you killed yourself because of me. I won't tolerate it, or your disgraceful deception. The moment you gave your word to marry me you were mine and I intend to collect. If you don't cooperate not only will I drug you, but I will kill your half-breed.'

This gave Little Sun pause. She turned her head to look at Blue Sky with wide, uncertain eyes. He tried to strangle out a warning that they were going to kill him anyway, that she shouldn't sacrifice anything for him, but it was no use. His words came out as muffled nonsense.

'So what's it going to be, sweet?' Gaunt asked. 'Come willingly or watch your Indian lover die?'

# CHAPTER TWENTY THREE

ilda tore her eyes away from Blue Sky and looked into Marcus's cold, dark pupils. How had she not seen when they first met how unfeeling they were? Perhaps because then she had never looked into the passionate depths of Blue Sky's eyes.

She took a deep breath and then, as Lawson's whisky-stench filled her lungs, at once regretted it. Arabella had returned to Widow Westerby's while Gilda was saddling up to say the letter had been passed on to Elise. Surely it was just a matter of time before Clarke arrived? Even if he didn't care to save Blue Sky's life, she had delivered his firstborn just three nights ago. He should at the very least come for her. She needed to bide more time.

'Very well,' she said. 'I will come with you back to England and will do so voluntarily.

But on one condition. As I shall live out my days in England and never see him again, I want to say goodbye to Blue Sky. Properly.'

Gaunt eyed Gilda for a moment and then glanced at Blue Sky. 'You have two minutes,' Gaunt said, before nodding at Lawson to release her.

Straightening herself up after Lawson's manhandling, Gilda marched over to Blue Sky. Looking at what they had done to him because of her she wanted to cry. His left eye was swollen and there was scarcely an inch of his face without a bruise. How selfish she was to get involved with him. He looked broken. Still, there was a chance they weren't going to get out of this and she'd be damned if the last thing he was going to see was her weeping. He had spent his life being brave for his people, now it was her turn to be brave for him.

Once before him, she gently removed the stretch of fabric they had used as a gag.

His face contorted in anguish. 'Little Sun, why did you come?'

'I – nearly didn't,' she answered honestly. 'I was terrified. I was almost in the coach out of town when I realised nothing scared me more than the possibility of never seeing you again.'

She ran her fingertips along the side of his face, being careful to skirt the cuts and bruises his captors had inflicted before gently kissing his lips and pressing her tongue against his. Her every movement was soft, careful, so as not to cause him anymore pain than she already had.

When they parted, their breath ragged in a mixture of desire and despair, Blue Sky leant his forehead against hers and whispered. 'Do not go with them Little Sun, they will kill me anyway. They have admitted as much.'

Gilda sneaked a hand into her dress pocket. With Gaunt and Lawson standing to her right they didn't see the shiny object she had retrieved before wrapping her arms around Blue Sky. 'Not if I can help it,' she whispered, letting her hands slip down to his. She palmed him a scalpel she'd brought from her medical bag and guided his fingers to the sharp edge so he would understand he now had a means of escape.

'Two minutes is up, get over here,' Gaunt yelled. When Gilda didn't at once comply, Lawson lolloped over, pistol in hand.

'Didn't you hear?' Lawson said, dragging her back into his clutches. 'Or maybe you're just too damn dumb to understand your predicament. I thought doctors were supposed to be smart.'

Lawson was so busy insulting Gilda, he didn't see her again reach into her pocket and grip a pair of medical scissors tight in her fist. He was unprepared then when she turned to him with all her might and stabbed the scissors straight through his thigh.

Blood gushed from the wound at once. Lawson screamed and his arms flailed.

'Don't even think about it, sweet,' Gaunt bit out, but Gilda paid him no heed. Lawson had loosened his grip on the pistol just enough to wrestle it from him. As soon as she had it she ran straight to where Blue Sky was still tied and stood poised with the pistol, guarding him.

'You're going to pay for that you little bitch,' Lawson spat. He grunted as he pulled the scissors from his thigh and cast them into the long grasses.

'One gun, one bullet loaded, two opponents,' Gaunt taunted, walking towards her. 'The odds do not seem in your favour. Even if you do hit one of us, the other will be left standing. Now hand me that gun before you hurt yourself.'

Gilda cocked the gun and aimed it squarely at Gaunt. He signalled for Lawson to stop moving. Gilda smiled. She had a feeling Gaunt might tread more lightly when there was a weapon trained on him.

'I will shoot you Marcus. For my father. For Blue Sky. For everything you've done to me. One more step and you will not see another sunrise.'

'But then I'll kill you and the half-breed,' said Lawson. 'Can't have any witnesses onto Mr Clarke about my part in all this.'

'It's a little late for that, Lawson,' a familiar voice called from the foliage. Mr Clarke emerged and Gilda glanced over to see he had Lawson covered with his pistol. He'd brought two other men from the town who Gilda vaguely recognised as being present in the market place on the day she had first arrived in Williamsburg. They also had pistols loaded and aimed in the direction of her tormentors. She had never been so relieved to see anyone in her entire life as she was to see Mr Clarke just now. The time had come to end this… once and for all.

Clarke must have edged close enough to see Gilda's finger closing on the trigger.

'Miss Griffiths, we're here now. Lower that gun.'

Gilda didn't pull the trigger any further but she didn't release it either.

'Miss Griffiths, put that pistol down!' Clarke bellowed. 'Mr Gaunt here is going to be tried for his crimes. You don't need to kill him.'

'He killed *my* father,' Gilda choked out while tears trailed down her cheeks.

'If that's the case, he won't escape the noose,' said Clarke.

'He… raped me,' Gilda whimpered.

There was a silence before Clarke spoke again. 'I know you're hurtin' Gilda but you need to let me handle this.'

Gilda knew she should do as she was told but in her mind's eye all she could see was the hurt Marcus had caused. The ruthless ways he had stripped her of her dignity. The casual fashion in which he had admitted to murdering her father, while in the same breath threatening to do the same to Andrew. And then there was Blue Sky. Because of him, Blue Sky might never trust another white person for as long as he lived, and Gilda couldn't blame him. She tightened her finger on the trigger but suddenly a firm and heavy hand fell on her shoulder.

Her bodily response to that touch told her, at once, that it was Blue Sky. He had broken free of his bonds and was at her side. Keeping the gun squarely pointed at Gaunt she looked up at him, at his battered face and chopped hair, and prepared to shoot. Before she could however, Blue Sky did the last thing she ever expected. He put his hand on top of the pistol and pushed down, forcing her to lower her weapon.

'What are you doing?' she pleaded. 'You know he deserves it. Let me do this. Let me kill him.'

'If you cross this line you will regret it. It will change you. You do not end life, Little Sun,' he managed to say, even through the pain. 'You save lives. You saved mine.'

Breathless, Gilda dropped the gun and reached out to embrace him but as she did so, Gaunt charged towards them wielding a knife he must have kept hidden in his coat pocket.

'Let her be, savage! She's mine,' he screamed. 'Mine!'

Gilda clung to Blue Sky but before Gaunt could reach them a shot rang out and Gaunt hurled sideways into the grass. Gilda took a couple of steps towards his motionless body; he had been shot clean through the head. She turned to see Mr Clarke lowering his pistol with a grave look on his face.

Gilda turned back to Blue Sky but he was not there. He was lying limp on the ground, likely overcome by his many wounds. At once, Gilda ran to kneel by his side, cradling his head in her arms. Somewhere in the periphery, she could hear Clarke and his men closing in on Lawson but every drop of her concentration was consumed with one critical duty: keeping her Blue Sky alive.

# CHAPTER TWENTY-FOUR

**B**lue Sky perched in a mahogany arm-chair in Mr Clarke's sitting room. He was convinced it was the most uncomfortable place he had ever had the misfortune to sit but perhaps that had more to do with the topic of conversation, and his attire.

When Blue Sky had requested Arabella buy him a shirt from a merchant in town, Gilda didn't see why they should spend money on clothes just to give a statement to Mr Clarke. He had, with what little strength remained in him, teased her that she preferred him without a shirt as a way to mask how important it was to him that on this matter the white men took him seriously. If that meant wearing their clothes for an afternoon, so be it.

'Between your statement and that of Miss Griffiths, Mr Lawson will be looking at the noose,' Clarke said.

'I am glad to hear justice will be served,' said Blue Sky. Though secretly, Blue Sky admitted he was not as glad as he thought he would be. Since meeting Little Sun he had begun to wish there was a way of living without killing others all the time.

Clarke nodded and eyed Blue Sky in a way that turned his stomach. 'This is probably none of my business,' the man said. 'But can I ask what you plan to do where Miss Griffiths is concerned?'

Blue Sky's body tensed. Since the showdown with Gaunt and Lawson four nights ago, he and Gilda had not discussed the future. He had tried on more than one occasion but she had quieted him, insisting they would talk when he had healed. She hadn't said as much but he got the sense that she expected him to leave once he was well. That perhaps he only used the last of his strength to plant affectionate kisses on her hand and trail his fingertips along her cheeks because he was grateful for her medical expertise. As he had lay in the spare room at the yellow house, while she tended him like the mother he had lost, he could not bring himself to entertain the alternative: that her experience with Gaunt had caused her to shy from men and that she was only healing him so that she might feel better about pushing him away after the fact.

'Things are uncertain,' said Blue Sky.

'Are they now?' Clarke said, rubbing his auburn beard. 'I will admit, that I cannot help but feel part way responsible for what happened to you both. If I had sanctioned Lawson more severely for his... treatment of your father, he might have thought twice about going into league with Gaunt. It is this sense of duty that compels me to show you the letter that Miss Griffiths sent to me the day she came after you.'

Clarke picked up one of the papers sitting on the small table next to his chair and handed it to Blue Sky. He looked at the paper, but could only make out a few words.

'Though I speak your language well enough, I do not read much English,' he admitted, handing it back to Clarke. He assumed that would be the end of the matter but Clarke sighed and began to recite what was written on the page.

*Mr Clarke,*

*By the time you read this letter I will be on my way to the spot marked on the map below to save Blue Sky's life. He is being held hostage by a dangerous man named Marcus Gaunt, and I believe Mr Lawson. Mr Gaunt is the reason I left England. I was supposed to marry him but his numerous cruelties were too much to bear. Mrs Clarke is lucky to have a man who treats her as well as you do. Not all women in England have that luxury, and I am afraid I am one of the many who have suffered at the hands of men who are supposed to honour them.*

*Despite my best efforts to cover my tracks, Gaunt has somehow followed me here and has learned of my fondness for Blue Sky. If I do not go to him I am certain Blue Sky will be dead by daybreak.*

*I do not expect you to understand my unconventional affections for a man I have just met, nor my need to risk my life for his. I admit to you plainly that it defies all logic. All*

*I can tell you is that I have never felt about anyone the way I do about this man. Unlike your fair Mrs Clarke, I cannot bear children and with my father gone and my brother three thousand miles away, he is the closest thing I have to family. I cannot stand by and let him die on my account. I must go to him. If it comes to it, I must use my last breath to save him.*

*I have heard the whispers in the short time I've been in Williamsburg. I know that the native people are not held in high regard but I implore you to put aside these idle prejudices and come to our aid. Regardless of what you may think, Blue Sky is a good man, the best I have met, and he is more worthy of your service than you will ever know.*

*Sincerely*

*Gilda Griffiths*

Blue Sky could barely breathe, or believe what he was hearing. Not only had his Little Sun made a plea for his life to a white man of power, she had declared her affections for him knowing that Clarke could have made their relationship public, and perilous, just by talking to the wrong person.

An indescribable warmth spread through him and in that moment he could deny to himself no longer that he was falling in love with this woman.

'I can't tell you what to do, Blue Sky. If Miss Griffiths chooses to be with you she will have a very hard life. But it is her choice and from what I know of her, if she does choose to be with you, I think you would be a foolish man to let her go. Granted, she can't bear you an heir but I get the feeling that in her prolonged company, you may soon forget that.'

Blue Sky nodded. He did not care about an heir. He did not care about having anything else, if he could just have her. 'I have no intention of letting her go,' he said to Clarke. He wouldn't normally share anything with a white man, but Clarke had not been forced to share Little Sun's letter with him, or come and rescue them four nights ago. He had admitted his wrongdoing and acknowledged how he had failed in his responsibilities. That took courage. At the very least, Blue Sky owed him the courtesy of polite treatment.

'In that case,' Mr Clarke said, a small smile on his lips. 'I should explain that there are some expectations when it comes to the courting of ladies such as Miss Griffiths. I daresay you have your own ideas but if you want to show her you are serious about a partnership, there are some things you need to know.'

'Tell me,' Blue Sky demanded. 'For her, I will do whatever it takes.'

# CHAPTER TWENTY-FIVE

ilda was wriggling her bare toes in the crisp waters of the James River when she heard him call her name.

'Little Sun…'

She at once turned from her seat on the river bank to see if he was really there. Once standing, she put her hands on her hips. 'What are you doing on a horse? You're in no condition.'

He dismounted and tethered his ride before walking over to her. 'I am much improved thanks to your nursing. Arabella said you had ridden out here and I could not wait to talk to you.'

'I'm sorry to have caused you the journey. I didn't know how long you would be with Clarke and,' she admitted, 'I couldn't find enough chores to busy myself around the house.' As she spoke she tried not to openly stare at him in his new linen shirt. She had been against him putting on any airs and graces for Clarke's sake but now that she saw him in the garment it was difficult not to imagine tearing it off him, and in turn difficult to decide whether this idea was more or less alluring than his bared chest alone.

'Mr Clarke did not keep me longer than necessary,' he said, to regain her full attention. The knowing smirk on his face made her wonder if he could read her mind.

'Hopefully our statements will be the end of the matter,' Gilda said, unable to stop herself from wondering, even as she said this, if it would ever truly be over for her.

Moving closer, he traced his fingertips along her cheek. 'It will take time for us both to heal. But we will, my Little Sun.'

'You... do still think of me as your Little Sun, then?'

Without a word he took both of her hands in his and slowly dropped to his knees.

'That is what I want. For us to belong to one another.'

Gilda's mouth fell open and her heart beat faster in her chest. So hard was the drumming she thought she might burst.

'I know you have been through a great ordeal,' he continued, 'and you have suffered things I may never fully understand. But I want to try. I want to listen. I want to protect you. If you will let me, I want to love you.'

'I want to love you too, if you will let me,' Gilda said, her tone soft and dreamy.

'When we met I wouldn't have known how to let you close,' he said. 'But my time with you has changed that. I've changed.'

'I can see that,' she said. 'There is a light in your eyes that wasn't there before.'

'I kneel before you to show you that if you choose a life with me I will always place your safety and happiness above my own. I will respect you, and care for you and treat you with the kindness you have shown me.'

Gilda dropped to her knees, joining him. Part because she wanted to return the gesture, part because she could no longer stay on her feet with such elation and astonishment raging through her. 'As I will you, my precious man,' she managed to say. 'As I will you.'

The thought of belonging to him and he to her, sparked an urgent need to be as close to him as she possibly could. More than anything, she longed for Blue Sky to, at last, take her with the fierce intensity promised during the time they had spent in each other's arms. But instead he spoke again.

Blue Sky's eyes lowered. 'I spoke to Mr Clarke about what our future may hold. I know it is too soon to speak of weddings but I must tell you: I cannot give you a marriage as you understand it my Little Sun. Mr Clarke explained that a formal union between us would not be recognised by your people. But that is not true of mine. If there comes a time when you want me for the rest of your days, my people have customs that make it binding, at least in the eyes of the Shawnee.'

Gilda could not hide her surprise, not just at his words but at the feelings that surfaced within her. After the pain and anguish she had experienced at the hands of her last suitor, she would have expected marriage to be the furthest thought from her mind. And yet, as she looked into his ocean-deep eyes, all she could imagine was his arms around her, his lips against her lips, his body on top of hers, forever.

'You would want to marry me, even though I cannot bear you a child?' she said, allowing her one last shred of doubt get the better of her.

'I cannot offer you a white marriage, you cannot offer me a child. Does it matter to you? All that matters to me, is being with you,' he returned.

'I feel the same,' she said, stroking the side of his jaw.

He smiled. 'So you will be with me?'

'Yes, with all my heart, yes,' she whispered.

The force of his kiss was enough to knock her backward into the long grasses and she kissed him back just as fiercely. For the past four days all she had focused on was his healing. Certain, despite his occasional soft touches, that once she had aided him he would not want any more to do with her after all she had cost him. But she had been wrong. He wanted her just as she wanted him.

She moaned at the feel of his weight on top of her and realised for the first time the unique pleasure simple pressure brought. Perhaps it was because she had had to traverse a whole continent to find him. Or that the fear over her ordeal with Gaunt hadn't quite dissipated and part of her still expected to have to pick up and leave for New Orleans at a moment's notice. Beneath the weight of his body however, that uneasy, untethered feeling evaporated. She knew he had strength enough to hold onto her and that she would never let him go. That thought alone had her tugging impatiently at the hem of his shirt.

Growling, he broke the kiss and pulled back. 'I must control myself.'

'What? Why?' Gilda asked, she could hear the petulance in her tone and didn't care. She had been denied the relief of feeling him inside her for too long. She thought she might die with the agony of how much she wanted him.

'Mr Clarke offered me some... advice,' said Blue Sky. 'It is clear that some things are meant to be left at least until we are living beneath the same roof.'

Gilda huffed out a sigh. If it wouldn't be the most uncomfortable conversation she had ever had, she would give Mr Clarke a piece of her mind for forcing the ideals of white society on Blue Sky. Especially those that further delayed his taking of her.

'You're not really going to let the stuffy words of an aging white man stand between us, are you?' she said with an impish smile. She did not want to tame his wild. More than anything, she wanted to run with it. 'We don't have a house we can call our own and who knows how long it might take to find one?'

Blue Sky chuckled, shaking his head at her efforts to tempt him. 'You leave that to me my Little Sun. And do not fear. Between now and then I will find other ways to remind you why we make such a good match.'

Gilda was about to tell him she would never need such a reminder but stopped short when she felt his hands slowly drifting up her thigh.

'Well, I can be dreadfully forgetful,' she said, just before his fingers met their mark.

# CHAPTER TWENTY-SIX

Ten days later, Blue Sky hammered the last of the nails into a cabin made of chopped cedar which, with the permission of Mr Clarke and the help of Fast River, he had built in a small clearing in the woods. Sweat beaded across his forehead as he worked. With every raise of the axe and every pound of the hammer he had thought of nothing else except the look of quiet pleasure he anticipated on Little Sun's face when he surprised her with their new home.

The cabin was not as large as the houses in the town but it was big enough for the two of them to eat and sleep. He had screened off a special room and constructed a small writing desk within so that Little Sun might be able to read and make her medical notes. He had also paid special attention to the building of their bed, where, he imagined, they would spend many torrid nights and lazy days learning the truths of each other's bodies. He had built the bed to be much wider than the one he had slept in at the Widow Westerby's, and tasked the women of his village to stuff and sew a thick mattress with a mix of buffalo and horse hair. He wanted it to be the most comfortable bed she had ever known. If the furnishings weren't enough to accomplish that he believed the offering of his body would make up for any shortcomings. And now that she had agreed to stay with him there would be no silk sheaths for them. He would take her bare and raw, just as he had wanted from the start.

'Blue Sky, you asked for me?' Great Hawk's voice sounded out behind him in their native tongue. Given the nature of his thoughts he was startled by his father's sudden presence but soon recovered himself.

Placing his tools down on the porch, Blue Sky walked over to greet Great Hawk who, he was pleased to see, had finally healed enough to travel on horseback.

His father had been nothing short of over-joyed when Blue Sky had told him of his partnership with Little Sun. But soon he would leave his village to live with her and before that happened there were some things he needed to say.

Once dismounted, Great Hawk looked the cabin up and down. 'You have built Little Sun a fine home. I am proud of you, my son.'

'I am pleased to hear it, father,' Blue Sky replied, his smile fading as he chose his next words carefully. 'But I called you here because before I can build a life with Little Sun, I need to ask you for something.'

'Anything,' Great Hawk said with a frown. Blue Sky understood his father's confusion. He had not asked Great Hawk for anything in as long as he could remember, even when he had badly needed help. For better or for worse he had always found his own way out of whatever scrapes he got himself into. But this was something only Great Hawk could grant.

'I want to ask for your forgiveness, father.' A lump formed in Blue Sky's throat. It felt as though he had learned more about himself in the last three weeks than he had in the last ten years. Perhaps this is what it meant to become a man. To strive to learn more about yourself with each passing day, so one might do better.

'Forgiveness?' Great Hawk said, his frown deepening. 'For what wrong?'

'When Lawson and Gaunt had me tied to that stake, I had to watch on helpless as they threatened and mauled my Little Sun,' Blue Sky explained. 'I thought surely they would kill her before I broke free of the bonds and no matter how much I struggled, I could do nothing to stop them. I have since realised that you know this pain. It was how you felt when they took my mother.'

Great Hawk's eyes glazed with tears. He was silent for a moment before speaking. 'One of the hardest things to accept is that we cannot protect those we love from everything that might harm them. Charlotte was a brave woman. Sometimes I believe that in addition to her eyes, you inherited her bravery, more so than you inherited it from me.'

'I cannot believe that. You have survived so much pain, and I have added to it.' Blue Sky placed a hand on his father's shoulder and squeezed. He couldn't remember the last time he had touched his father this way, with vulnerability and affection. Possibly not since he was a small boy. 'I am sorry for leaving you alone with your hurt all these years. I am able to listen now, to the things I could not hear before. If you ever need me.'

Great Hawk studied Blue Sky with large watery eyes. 'A father always needs his son.' The two men took a deep breath in such synchrony that it almost seemed that they were breathing as one. Unable to stop himself, Blue Sky leaned forward and put his arms around his father. Hoping Great Hawk could feel whatever part of his mother still lived in him in the embrace. They stayed that way for a minute or two before parting. Great Hawk put a hand to his son's scarred cheek and Blue Sky, for the first time, really let himself notice the love in the old man's eyes.

'Can I offer you a piece of advice, my son?' Blue Sky nodded his approval.

'If she had not loved me, Charlotte would have grown old but there is a difference between staying alive and truly living. Little Sun has chosen a life with you because she loves you but that life will not be an easy one. She is intelligent and will already know this but make sure you give her a life that is worth that sacrifice.'

'I will do everything I can to please her, father, I promise.'

Blue Sky watched a single tear sneak down his father's cheek, and made a silent vow that his story with Little Sun would not end in the same way Great Hawk's had with Charlotte. In honouring his Little Sun he would honour his lost mother and make the most of the happiness that had been bestowed upon him. The happiness he knew in his heart his mother would want for her son, even if she was not here in body to witness it.

# CHAPTER TWENTY-SEVEN

ittle Sun. That was her name now. It was official, well as official as she could hope to make it.

Over the past fortnight she had instructed all who came into contact with her to call her by that name. Though Arabella had let slip that she had shouted down more than one snide remark behind her back in that time, nobody had dared call her Gilda to her face. Gilda Griffiths, much like Briar Chatterton, was a name that belonged to another time now. A time before she knew what it truly meant to feel safe and cherished in the arms of a man who loved her.

As instructed by Blue Sky, she had taken her ride along the road to his village. She was half way from town when she saw him, standing bare-chested at the side of the road in his buckskins and a black breechcloth. Smiling, she steered the horse towards him and chuckled as he pulled a bunch of bluebells from behind his back. The first of the season she had seen.

Dismounting, she hastened to kiss him and run her fingers through his midnight hair which, although still not back to its original length, was growing longer at a pleasing rate.

'Hmmm. Between the flowers, the hair braiding and the meal you cooked for me three nights ago, I think you are being terribly unfair.'

'Unfair, how?' he asked, his eyes twinkling.

'You know how badly I want you and how torturous it has been to wait. You shouldn't really be doing any more nice things for me until the wait is over. It only makes it… harder,' she said, her eyes gliding over his bronzed chest all the way down to his breechcloth.

He leaned into her then, brushed her hair behind her ear and whispered. 'It has been sweet torture for me too, my Little Sun, but the wait is over.'

Little Sun's breath caught in her throat. 'Truly?'

'Truly,' he said, handing her the Blue Bells before scooping her up in his arms.

'Blue Sky, you mustn't. Your wounds,' she said, concerned for a moment that he might not be able to bear her weight when he was yet to regain his full strength. His plight was not without obvious effort but he summoned the might to carry her down a narrow path into the trees. They soon broke out into a small clearing where a wooden cabin stood. Her heart swelled as she looked at it. A step led up to a small porch with a bench to sit on. A lantern hung by the door and come night fall, Little Sun imagined, it would flicker with a dreamy orange glow.

'What do you think?' Blue Sky said, nodding at the cabin.

'I think it's the quaintest home I've ever seen. Is it ours?'

'Yes, I built it for us.'

'You – you *built* it?' Little Sun gaped. 'How? When?'

'I started work as soon as you agreed to be with me. Knowing I could not lie with you until it was done was more than enough motivation to work at speed.'

Little Sun's first response was to laugh but then her smile faded. 'You should not be working your body so hard. You shouldn't really be lifting a weight like me! You are barely healed.'

'I would use my dying breath to lift you into my arms,' he said, and she cursed the fact that his words were too romantic to logically argue with. 'Do not fear. Fast River helped me build the cabin,' he added. 'Though if he tries to take all of the credit do not pay him much heed.'

Little Sun laughed. 'Oh, my Blue Sky. I never expected this.'

'I know, that is how surprises work.'

She tapped him playfully on the chest, though she let her hand linger a little longer there than necessary.

'It stands exactly half way between my village and your town,' he said. 'It is to show you that, though we are from different worlds, I will meet you half way in all things.'

She bit her lip and stared at him. 'Then I shall meet you more than half way just to out-do you.'

Blue Sky let out a deep, rich laugh that Little Sun decided she would do everything in her power to hear more often. 'We will live between the worlds,' he said, 'but we will do so with love in our hearts.'

She looked again at the cabin, imagining their life together. It had been agreed that Arabella would stay with Widow Westerby – who was more than glad of the company – so it would just be the two of them, whenever Arabella wasn't visiting to fulfil her duties as maid.

She turned back to gaze at Blue Sky's precious face. Unable to resist any longer, Little Sun pulled his head to hers and kissed him with every ounce of might. Before she knew what was happening, Blue Sky had marched her to the porch. He nudged open the door with his foot and passed over the threshold.

Slowly, he dropped her to her feet then, allowing her to take in their new home.

Her gaze flitted over the hundred or more tiny comforts he had arranged for her. A writing desk, complete with parchment and ink. A pile of furs rolled next to the fire place. A tin tub for bathing. 'Where did you get the chairs?' she asked.

'Mr Clarke had them to spare. The women of the village sewed the cushions. But I am more interested in showing you the bedroom,' Blue Sky replied, grabbing her hand and turning into a room that contained the biggest bed she had ever seen.

Blue Sky stood in front of the bed. For a moment she contemplated pushing him backwards onto it and straddling him. Something in his eyes however kept her rooted to the spot. He began to circle her in much the way she imagined a wolf might circle its prey. On the first pass, he surveyed her with such hunger that she could barely breathe for her excitement. On his second pass, he stopped just behind her, placed his hands on her hips and pulled her body hard against his.

'The lady wanted me to undress her, I seem to remember,' he said. She felt his hands pull slowly at the laces on her dark green dress. The same dress she had worn the day they had met.

Softly, she moaned as the tension in the corset gave and his roughened hands pushed the garment from her shoulders. He pulled at the cords on her petticoats and in an instant they all fell away so that she stood in nothing but her shift, her stockings and her boots. The next thing she felt were his firm hands clasped about her ankles, angling underneath her shift and rising, rising past her stockings to her thighs, then her buttocks, then her waist, then her breasts.

Little Sun swallowed hard. Trying in vain to even out her erratic breathing. Blue Sky whipped the shift off over her head so that that only her boots and stockings remained.

'You are beautiful,' he growled close to her ear. She could not see his face but she felt the heat of his gaze on her every rear curve. His lips met the back of her neck and her body arched in response. His every caress was so brutally tender it both reassured and thrilled her. No man had ever touched her this way. He kissed his way down her spine, just as he had promised he would that morning they had lain in the woods together. When his lips arrived at her waist, he reached a hand up to the top of her back and pressed firmly, bending her forwards over the bed. Her breathing quickened as he grabbed her buttocks in his firm hands, parted them and continued to trail his tongue over her most intimate nooks.

'Oh Blue Sky,' she whimpered, as he greedily nudged her legs further apart to gain better access.

'I will never tire of the taste of you,' he paused to say. To prove it, he continued to thrash his tongue over every available inch of skin until her body shook and writhed.

'Blue Sky, please,' she begged. 'After waiting so long, I can't take much more and I want to reach my peak with you inside me.'

He continued to lick her for a few more moments, unwilling to yield his position so easily but then, seemingly taken with the image of her climaxing while his rod was buried deep inside her, he stood, pulled her up from her previous position and turned her to face him. She could see the want in those ocean-deep eyes and had no doubt that he saw the same in hers. Without a word, he closed his arms around her and lay her gently down on the softest bed she had ever known.

Their bed. In this house, which he had built for them.

As soon as she was settled, he pulled off her boots and untied the ribbons on her stockings before tearing them away so she lay there completely bared to him, waiting. The mere sight of her was enough to spur Blue Sky into shedding his own clothes with increasing haste. He kicked off his moccasins, threw off his belt, ripped off his buckskins and couldn't untie his breechcloth quick enough.

She stared at him in awe. It was the first time she had seen him utterly naked. Had the chance to marvel at the muscles rippling in his thighs, the right of which was marked with a crimson scar, or at how his dark hair grew thicker in some places than others. He looked to her like a dream. And she could hardly wait to spend the rest of her life exploring every peak and shallow of his sculpted form.

Gently, he positioned his body over hers. Bending his head down to kiss her, he quickly found her tongue and massaged it with his. She could taste herself on him. Could taste the boundless arousal he stirred in her, and as she opened her mouth wider, her thighs parted further for him also. She needed his tongue, his manhood, his whole being to fill the empty spaces within her.

Blue Sky required no further invitation and positioned himself at her entrance.

'So… wet…so… perfect,' he groaned as he eased his pole inside her, inch by inch.

'Yes… please… yes…' she wailed as he pushed deeper and deeper. She could feel his throbbing, it matched her own. He did not stop until he was sheathed to the hilt, at which point he lay still for a moment. Allowing her to adjust to his size and taking the opportunity to suck on the closest nipple, whilst lightly pinching the other. The roughness of his stubble against her breasts paired with the feeling of his hot length pulsing inside her, spurred Little Sun to drive her hips into his.

'I want you so much,' she whispered, just before Blue Sky returned his lips to hers, grunting into her mouth as he pushed her legs even wider. He placed a firm hand around her neck and squeezed just tight enough to hold her in place. She would not have expected to like this but some strange feeling of security stirred as his fingers gently fastened around her throat.

His rhythm started out slow. He pushed deep before pulling as far back as he could without disengaging before repeating this motion again. Filling her with long, deep strokes that she met with equal depth and strength.

For uncountable delirious moments, she was completely mesmerised by his movements and the almost tortured moans that came from him as he thrusted back and forth, in and out without any signs of slowing. His impressive stamina aroused her more than she could have imagined. It felt as though he might never stop and that idea drove her wild.

'Please, please, please Blue Sky, harder,' she moaned, wondering if it were possible for him to push any harder than he already was. Without a blink, he released his hand from her neck and raised her legs, grabbing her ankles and pushing them back towards her shoulders. This, she found, granted him the depth she had been craving. She whimpered as he continued to pound into her without pause or hesitation.

'Please, take me faster,' she cried, and again Blue Sky did not disappoint, ramming himself into her at what seemed like double the pace he had before. With every thrust her full breasts shook back and forth, and those tight sacks between his legs smacked against her skin. Something about the fast, unyielding nature of the sound took her pleasure to a height she had not known was even possible. Her thighs began to tremble in a way that suggested her zenith was near. Wanting to connect her skin to his in every possible place, she reached down and wrapped her arms around her lover so she could feel him grinding into her. The clenching of his hard buttocks beneath her hands was unlike anything she had ever felt before. She gripped him tighter and teased his opening with her fingertips.

'Oh Little Sun,' he hissed. Every muscle in his body seemed to constrict and though she would not have thought it possible he drove into her even harder than he had before. This sensation, along with the view of his sweating, muscular form heaving over her, was more than she could stand and she lurched upward, biting hard into his shoulder as a climax pulsed through her pinkened body.

Blue Sky was not far behind and in the space of a few further thrusts a sound that was part moan, part war cry echoed from his lips. An aftershock of bliss gripped her as she felt his hot seed burst deep inside.

Gasping, the pair collapsed into each other's arms. Blue Sky rolled his body to the side and then pulled her close. She nestled into him, wanting to cling to the euphoric intimacy she had just experienced.

'Was it all you imagined, my Little Sun?' he whispered as he kissed the side of her head.

'More,' she whispered in return. 'So much more.'

'Your skin is like the morning sky after love-making,' Blue Sky said, resting his head on her breasts. She held him close against her bosom, stroked his soft, inky hair and sighed. For the first time ever, she knew she was right where she was supposed to be. She kissed his forehead and her heart was filled with gratitude for the fact that, even if it had meant crossing an ocean, this Little Sun had found her Blue Sky.

For a free collection of romantic short stories set in vintage NYC please visit helencox-books.com/mailinglist

# ACKNOWLEDGMENTS

Heartfelt thanks to my historian of a husband Jo Pugh for his love, and support in rendering the historical aspects of this novella.

Thank you to Dean Cummings, Ann Leander, Katia Hernandez and Jeanie Robinson for their invaluable feedback on my story. Gratitude also to Hammad Khalid for his spectacular book design skills.

Without you all, my life as an author would be lonelier and a lot less colourful.

Printed in Great Britain
by Amazon